Out of Slavery:

A Novel of Harriet Tubman

CAROL TREMBATH

Acknowledgements

A book is never the solitary work of a single writer. This book stands on the foundation of information constructed by such great historians as David W. Blight, Kate Clifford Larson, Sarah Bradford, and others. The story of Out of Slavery: A Novel of Harriet Tubman, was fashioned into being by its editor Kristin Nitz and the professional services of Streetlight Graphics.

Out of Slavery: A Novel of Harriet Tubman
Copyright © 2019 by Carol A. Trembath All rights reserved.
First Edition: 2019

Paperback ISBN: 978-0-9907446-8-9

Cover and Formatting: Streetlight Graphics

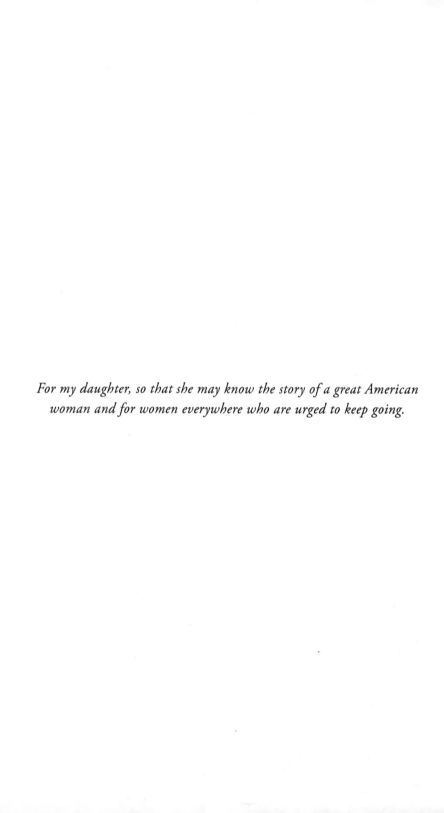

For my daughter, so that she may know the story of a great American woman and for women everywhere who are urged to keep going.

"Injustice anywhere is a threat to justice everywhere."
—*Dr. Martin Luther King, Jr.*

"Nothing is as powerful as an idea whose time has come."
—*Victor Hugo*

"It's a matter of taking the side of the weak against the strong, something the best people always have done."
—*Harriet Beecher Stowe*

"Four score and seven years ago our fathers brought forth on this continent, a new nation, conceived in Liberty, and dedicated to the proposition that all men are created equal."
—*President Abraham Lincoln*

Contents

Preface

Most of Harriet Tubman's early days on the plantation were made up of tedious routine and back-breaking work. But during the evening on November 12, 1833, the heavens seemed to open up as the annual Leonid meteor shower put on a particularly spectacular show. Thousands of shooting stars illuminated the night sky. For Harriet and her family, there was a sense this phenomenon might be a harbinger of some impending calamity. It was not long after this that Harriet received a near-fatal blow to her head. It changed the course of her life not only physically but spiritually as well.

After her near-death experience, Harriet's path changed. She was driven by her inner compass to work for freedom on a grand scale. After claiming first her own freedom, she turned back to take thirteen more trips south to rescue others caught in the web of slavery. Each person on her train to freedom represented a victory over tyranny and one more chorus of alleluia being heard in heaven.

Harriet was not only a cook, nurse, and spy during the Civil War, but also was the only woman to lead men into battle. This unprecedented event occurred during the daring raid up the Confederate held Combahee River in South Carolina. Harriet often fought and followed men into battle. She was a witness to the fight for Fort Wagner in Charleston, South Carolina and described it this way: "And then we saw the lightning, and that was the guns; and then we heard the thunder, and that was the big guns; and then we heard the rain falling, and that was the drops of blood falling; and when we came to get the crops, it was dead men we reaped."

Harriet was a fearsome, strong, and capable woman who was rooted in her goal to bring a light to others as she followed the North Star. Like so many other abolitionists and woman suffragettes of her times, Harriet knew that "free speech and slavery could not coexist for long in any society ... and the spirit—that would cut off free speech, was the spirit of slavery." Her friend Frederick Douglass warned of the same and said, "History was not merely an entity altered by the passage of time; it was a prize in the struggle between rival versions of the past, a question of will, of power, and of persuasion." Harriet's journey and the message of her life is told in the following pages. Her story will shine a light on the path she had chosen and the truth of her great heart.

Her tombstone in Auburn, New York reads:

"Servant of God, Well Done."

Chapter 1:
Uprooted

THERE ARE STORMS HERE IN Maryland, big racer storms. When it happens, the sky turns a sick yellow. The winds uproot trees, exposing their white roots. On a rainy, gray morning, I saw my big sister chained and sold south. I still recall Lindy's frightened and helpless face as she turned to look at my brother Lou and me for the last time. It was a forever good-bye because the word south carried the sound of doom. The Deep South meant cruelty. The Deep South meant early death.

A few months earlier my sister said, "Cece, I'm going to show you something, but you got to promise never to tell anyone or we'll both get whupped or worse. You know they learn from books in the master's house and I watch them over my shoulder. I ain't supposed to know words but I listen good and I'm gonna show you letters."

Behind our cabin at dusk, Lindy daily scratched words with a stick in the dirt. She taught me letters and words and I started walking and talking proud, like I was reading right off a paper. But it happened that I left the words, "see, water, run" outside by the side of our cabin one night. I didn't remember to brush the dirt clean. I forgot about the master forbidding us slaves from learning to read or write.

The next morning, I was gathering eggs in the chicken coop when I heard the screaming. I heard my sister yelling, "I did it. I did it. I made them words." The overseer had her by the hair and was dragging her toward the master's house. I ran to tell the overseer it was me that wrote down them words. I heard the crack of a whip and knew Lindy was getting hit.

In back of the main house by the cook's summer kitchen, I saw the overseer and the master. I saw blood dripping down my sister's face and arms. I tried to open my mouth, but fear squeezed my voice so tight that nothing came out. I wanted to say it was me. It was me that wrote them words. But my sister looked once at me with a warning look, shot straight from her brown eyes that always meant, "Not now".

"It's time to sell this one," the master said. "We don't want anyone else thinking they can learn to read and write around here. This one will be gone tomorrow."

Gone—that word echoed in my head. My sister was to be sold. The end came the next day as Lindy was led off in chains, just like it happened to my ma and pa a long time ago. I watched from the top of the fence, weeping till she was hidden from my sight forever. I felt a hopeless grief in my soul and that was the start of my uprooting. I knew I had to find a way to escape the plantation before my brother Lou and I shared the same fate.

Lou whispered the unthinkable first. "Cece, it's time for us to run away. I've heard there's freedom in the North. I heard tell that Harriet Tubman escaped from the Brodess Plantation just a few miles from here to a place called Pennsylvania. There's talk now that she came back last December and took with her a few slaves to safety on some underground railroad. I want to make my way to that train and get on board. I want to do this as soon as we can find that conductor."

I looked at Lou with my mouth wide-open and said, "Lou, I know you know that if we got caught they'd beat us with a whip, brand us with a runaway R, and sell us south. It would make your hair stand on end, knowing what they would do to us. But I'm glad you said it first, because I know we got to do this."

"I know a Quaker woman who said if I ever needed help about escaping, to let her know. Sometimes she rides in her wagon past where I work in the fields picking cotton. She's been saying there soon would a way out and she would tell me where to meet. I'm going to let her know we're ready."

News traveled fast on a downward wind and swept quickly from plantation to plantation. Before I knew it, a meeting time was arranged. Soon my brother and I were gathering food and a few belongings. We were on our way to meet the conductor named Harriet Tubman. Folks told us there was a reward of $1,200 for capturing her –dead or alive.

The meeting place was miles away from our plantation at the edge of the Greenbrier Swamp. Lou and I left after dark on Saturday night. No one worked on Sunday, so no one would miss us till Monday morning. The slave catchers and bloodhounds would be out after that. My body shook so bad I could barely walk straight. I tried to speak, but nothing came out just thinking about what I was doing.

I found the meeting place and we saw folks gathered under a giant cypress tree. There in the center was a woman scarcely five feet tall with wooly hair. She was holding a staff and carried a canteen and a haversack. She called out, "Are you Cecelia?"

"Yes, that's my name, ma'am, but they call me Cece. This is my brother, Lou."

"I am Harriet Tubman, and I will be conducting you north."

Then out of her pocket, Harriet flashed a pistol. She continued, "There will be no turning back now. If you're not strong enough to make the trek, you won't be strong enough to keep from telling the overseer when he starts whipping you about what we're doing here. If you change your mind, I will use this and you'll never take another step. You go on, or die."

Harriet went on, "It's several hundred miles to freedom. We'll be traveling by night, staying off the main roads and resting by day. Along the way there will be stations where a few kindly folks—

Quakers, whites, and black freemen—will be risking their lives and property for you. They'll be giving us food to eat and a place to hide. Slave catchers with guns will be patrolling trails and searching buildings along the way. So just do as I say. Follow me."

We traveled light and fast. We used rivers and small boats to take us to Maryland's Eastern Shore. Harriet knew all the places where it was safe to hide: drainage ditches, hedges, abandoned sheds, and tobacco barns. Even potato holes in the floors of farmer's homes were a good hiding place.

Harriet piloted us northward, but we were a trembling group. The sound of a moving animal or the flutter of leaves would cause our hearts to jump into our throats. Up and down the road Harriet would sneak past us to see if the coast was clear. She was always reading the forest to see if the slave catchers were pursuing us.

When we arrived at a safehouse, Harriet would hide us and knock at the door. When someone asked, "Who's there?" She would say the words, "A friend of a friend." But often our only bed was the cold ground as we followed the North Star.

We were near a farmer's field one night when Harriet suddenly motioned us to stop. She said she would go ahead and would come back for us when it was clear. Watching Harriet move slowly forward along the edge of the field, we could see that she suddenly fell down near a low ditch. Time passed and she lay motionless.

We were worried about Harriet. She had a trouble—a kind of sleeping sickness or blackouts. She would be in the middle of a sentence and then fall down into a deep sleep right along the trail. No one could wake her till her mind and body were ready.

She had told us, "I got hurt bad in the head when I was a young girl by a cruel foreman. My mama prayed hard so I am alive today. But I get these spells that come on quick and there is no telling when or for how long they'll last."

"What should we do?" my brother whispered. "We can't stay here on the edge of this field all night. The sun will be coming up soon. I don't think she's out there hiding. It looks like she might be suffering one of her ailments."

A tall man next to Lou nodded and said, "This doesn't look good. Let's skedaddle. We can't be too far from the border."

A young woman wearing a red bandana named Tilly whispered, "You're right, but how far would we get? We don't know the route. I tell you, I've been waiting a long time for a chance to meet up with Harriet Tubman—the Moses of our people. I ain't running off with nobody else except her."

"I think we should wait a while," I said. "No one knows the rivers and woods like Harriet. Someone might need to go out there and get her, but I'm for waiting."

Then a big man named Eli said, "I heard there's a lot of bounty hunters is this area. You know they will be out looking for us by now. I thought I heard some hounds a little way back. The idea of what they'd do to us if we get caught makes my skin crawl. I'm thinking we should make a run for it ourselves. Anyone with me?"

I said, "I'm not leaving here with Harriet out there in the dark. She brought us this far and she needs our trust. Lou, let's go and get her."

Right then I saw a shadow and heard the cock of a gun. A woman's voice said, "I carry this pistol for the faint of heart. If you decide to go off on your own, you die tonight. A dead fugitive tells no tales. Not all the tracks on the Underground Railroad run smooth. Never forget who your conductor is *me*—Harriet Tubman, and I am your only bridge to safety."

We were all shaken by Harriet's sickness and fateful warning, but relieved that she was back. We knew with her iron will she would get us to the Promise Land. At sunrise we rested in the shelter of a grove of low bending evergreens. We were as silent as death as Harriet hummed quiet church hymns that calmed our nerves.

After six days of hunger and cold, we made it across some invisible mark called the Mason-Dixon Line. Harriet knew the landmarks and one morning called out, "I want you to know that you're now in the land of the free. You won't be calling anyone Master, no more."

I hugged my brother and everyone shouted, "Glory, alleluia. We're free."

Harriet went on. "I want to say, when I found I had crossed that line for the first time, I looked at my hands to see if I was the same person. There was such glory over everything; the sun came like gold through the trees, and over the fields, and I felt like I was in heaven. A few more stops and we'll see folks who will take you in till you're able to live on your own. But right now, we are going to Rochester, New York to the home of Frederick Douglass. He's a great abolitionist and speaker for the cause of freedom. He's called by many folks, 'The Lion of Anacostia.' "

Two more days of travel and we were greeted by a tall, great lion of a man. His hair and beard ran around his face in one long mane. He was all the things a great lion would be: courageous, powerful, intelligent, and fierce, with a roaring voice of conviction. We spent just a few nights in his home. He and Harriet talked a long time that first night. It was my habit to stand close enough to hear, but not to be noticed.

I listened while Mr. Douglass told Harriet, "Congress passed the Fugitive Slave Act. It demands that people of the North return any fugitive slave. Now you and your passengers on the Underground Railroad are no longer safe here in the northern states. With this new law, slave catchers now have the legal right to arrest in northern states, without warning, any runaway slave and return them to their former enslavers. Anyone caught would see a fate worse than they could have ever dreamed of."

"Yes, I understand," answered Harriet. "I will be taking my passengers clear off to Canada where black people are free and have the same rights as whites. I won't be trusting Uncle Sam any more. From here, I'll be taking my passengers by train into Canada. Once that locomotive crosses the Niagara Falls Suspension Bridge, we'll be free."

"So, are you taking your passengers to St. Catharines, near Niagara Falls?"

"Yes," Harriet replied. "It used to be about 100 miles to get across the Mason-Dixon Line to freedom. Now with the Fugitive Slave Act, it's 450 miles to get to Canada. My passengers will be safe under the paw of the British lion and the rule of Queen Victoria. I've heard that the she has refused to allow U.S. officials to enter Canada and take back runaway slaves."

Harriet continued, "Years ago I was told that both my grandparents came here in chains from the warrior tribe of the Ashanti in West Africa. I tell you, I will fight for my people. When I learned that my master was going to send me south, I knew there was one of two things I had a right to, liberty or death. If I could not have one, I would have the other."

"You know you are being called the Moses of your people?" Mr. Douglass said.

"Yes, I've heard," Harriet replied, "but I remember the first time I crossed the Mason-Dixon Line. I was free, but there was no one to welcome me. I was a stranger here. My home, after all, was in Maryland. My father, my mother, my brothers, and my sisters were there. I wanted freedom for my family and the rest of my people. I'm gonna sing them north with all my breath—Let my people go."

Mr. Douglass shook his head, "You and I were slaves from neighboring counties in Maryland. We're a kind-of kin. But the difference between what we do is very different. Most that I have done and suffered in our cause has been in the public, and I have received much encouragement at every step of the way. I have wrought in the day—you in the night. I have had the applause of the crowd and the satisfaction of being approved by the multitude, while the most that you have done has been witnessed by a few trembling, scared, and foot-sore bondmen and women whose heartfelt, 'God bless you' has been your only reward."

"That might be true, Mr. Douglass. But, I don't need applause or approval. I only need freedom for my people. I know the weight of those shackles and chains has got to be broken."

Douglass nodded and said, "You have done so much. I am sure one day in heaven you will be lifted high. It's time for you now to go and gets some rest. You've got a long way yet to go. Safe travels, old friend."

Listening at the side of the parlor door, I knew I would be forever grateful to Harriet who brought my brother and me to the great state of New York, just like Moses brought slaves out of bondage from Egypt. The trek scared me to the bone, but Harriet was a good conductor. She held her pistol and wits about her at all times, so we made it through to the North.

Along our escape route, I saw wanted posters of Harriet. I knew that she did not know how to read or write. But I could make out some letters and words. Who Harriet really was, never fit the description that I saw on those ragged pieces of paper. They all missed telling about her great heart. She would never free a whole nation of slaves like Moses, but I knew she had the desire and the will to do so.

Chapter 2:
Stings Of Slavery

HARRIET BROUGHT MY BROTHER LOU and me out of a life of bondage. Survivors of the stings of slavery and the risky tests of runaways share a common chain. We are linked by suffering and an uncommon faith in each other. We become kinfolks. After our escape, all those in our fugitive party went north into Canada, but the Canadian winters were bitter cold. After several years, Harriet decided to relocate to Auburn, New York, with her rescued parents. Even though the Fugitive Slave Act was in force, Lou and I followed as well as Tilly. I started teaching Sunday school and Lou and Tilly began learning how to read and write from our minister.

Throughout the 1850s, Harriet struggled daily to make ends meet for herself and her family. Lack of money was her biggest worry and barrier to conducting more slaves to freedom. Years earlier Senator William Seward, seeing how desperate she was for funds, took it upon himself to purchase a seven-acre farm and house on the outskirts of Auburn, New York for her to live in.

At the time selling property to a known fugitive slave was against the law and he might have been arrested, but like so many others, he was a supporter of her cause. "Harriet," he said, "you have worked for others long enough. You never ask for anything for yourself. It is time to receive. All I ask is that you send me regular, small payments." Harriet was forever grateful.

For many years Harriet conducted fugitive slaves from Maryland into Canada. She also traveled the speaker circuit throughout New York and Boston seeking donations for telling her truth about slavery. To protect herself from possible slave catchers, she would often use the name of Harriet Garrison. Her abolitionist friends hoped she would help raise awareness for the cause of emancipation.

Tilly told me that Harriet was speaking at Seneca Falls just a little over twenty miles from Auburn. My brother, Tilly, and I decided to go and listen to the talk she was giving. When we went inside, Harriet recognized us right away and said, "Hello, Cece. Hello, Lou. Hello, Tilly. I hear you're doing well in Auburn. Glad you traveled here tonight. I could always use supporters. One day I would like to recruit all of you for the cause. Tonight, I hope these folks will listen and understand the terrors and violence of slavery."

"I do believe they will," I said, "because you'll be speaking from your heart and you're pretty frank and honest."

That night Harriet talked to a packed house of anti-slavery folks. I knew her words would shatter the audience's beliefs about quaint plantation life. Those attending were eager to hear more of her story. However, no one expected this plainly dressed black woman of small stature to have such a presence. We knew her deep, strong voice would soon shake the room. As she began, the three of us sat near the back of the hall and listened.

Harriet began, "I've heard *Uncle Tom's Cabin* read, and I tell you Mrs. Stowe's pen hasn't begun to paint what slavery is as far as I have seen it in the far South. I've seen the real thing. I've heard the shrieks and cries of women being flogged in the Negro quarter. Every time I saw a white man, I was afraid of being carried away. I listened many times to the groaned-out prayer, 'Oh Lord, have mercy.' As a child I was hired out by my master many times to other owners and was repeatedly whipped including a time I was beaten for some trivial offense by a man using a knot at the end of a rope, breaking my ribs."

Harriet continued, "The enslavers worked us worse than the animals. I started working in the fields, then in timber yards and docks with my father because it was a way of escaping the tyranny of demanding, cruel mistresses and the advances of the masters. I became so strong that a master I worked for in the timber business, thought of me something like a showpiece. He would show me off to his friends while I demonstrated my feats of strength. I could cut half a cord of wood in a day, more than most men. I prayed to God to make me strong and able to fight and that's what I've prayed for ever since."

Harriet then pointed to her brow. "You might've noticed the gash in my forehead. When I was a young girl about twelve or thirteen, the plantation's cook and I went to the nearby dry goods store for items for the house. On the way, I saw an overseer chasing after a runaway slave named Barnett. He ran inside the dry goods store to hide, but the overseer was right behind him.

"I began running after both of them and when I got inside the store, the overseer told me to hold onto that man, so that he could tie him up for whipping. I refused. When Barnett bolted, I put myself between him and the overseer.

"That overseer was so angry, that he picked up a two-pound weight and threw it after that runaway slave. It missed him and hit me square in the head. The last thing I remember was the overseer raising his arm up to throw that weight, and that was all I knew. The cast-iron weight broke my skull and cut a piece of the shawl that I was wearing around my head, clean off and drove it into my head. I dropped like a stone and I was carried back to my parents' cabin.

"After two days with no medical attention, I was sent right back out into the field to work. With the heat of the day, the sweat and blood started pouring down my face till I couldn't see no more and I fell down in the dirt. They carried me back home. My mother stopped the bleeding, but I drifted in and out of consciousness, from Christmas till March."

Harriet shook her head and went on, "After that my master wanted me sold. Prospective buyers would come by to look at me lying motionless on a bed of rags in the corner of my family's windowless wooden cabin. No one would even pay a sixpence for me. My parents though, possessed a strong faith and prayed hard for my recovery. But that illness also kept me from being sold and taken away from my parents. Lying on the cold, damp floor of the cabin, I'd say, 'Oh, dear Lord, I ain't got no friend but you. Come to me for I'm in trouble.'

"After the long illness, a deep religious spirit came over me. It was something that I never experienced before. I was suddenly praying all the time. I was always talking to the Lord. I went to the horse trough to wash my face and took up the water in my hands. I said, 'Oh Lord, wash me, make me clean.' When I would take out the broom and begin to sweep the floor, I groaned, 'Oh Lord, whatever sins there be in my heart, sweep it out, Lord, clear and clean.' "

A lady in the front row asked, "What do you think of slavery, Harriet?"

Harriet frowned and said, "My cry to slaveholders has always been, 'Let my people go.' I think slavery is the next thing to hell. If a person would send another into bondage, he would, it appears to me, be bad enough to send him into hell if he could. Now I've been free, I know what a dreadful condition slavery is. I have seen hundreds of escaped slaves, but I never saw one who was willing to go back and be a slave."

A person near the back row asked, "Harriet, what made you decide to run away?"

Harriet answered, "A strong vision came to me in a dream. I saw hands that beckoned me to be calm and were showing me a line dividing the land of slavery and the land of freedom. On the other side of that line were lovely flowers and a beautiful white lady waiting to welcome me. When I heard that my master was going to sell me south, I knew I had to take the risk and make a run for freedom. I made it into Pennsylvania with the help from many kind conductors on the Underground Railroad."

Several hands went up. One person shouted, "Can you tell us, Mrs. Tubman, what the Underground Railroad is?"

Harriet hesitated and then said, "I can't tell you all that I know about it because it is a secret organization, but in truth, it is not a real railroad with tracks and trains. It is a loose network of safehouses and transportation provided by free blacks, Quakers, and abolitionists. Usually a safehouse owner does not know the entire network, just a few connecting stations. People who work the Underground Railroad are known as agents, conductors, engineers, or stationmasters. I am a conductor."

Another person asked, "So Harriet, what made you decide to go back to rescue your family and other folks?"

Harriet looked wistful, saying, "I realized that freedom did not guarantee happiness. I was free, but I decided that my parents and family should be free too. So I began my journeys back south. But the bigger question in my mind began to spin, 'Why should such things be? Is there no deliverance for my people?' So began my passion to lead as many slaves as I could from the land of bondage to the land of freedom."

Another man in the front row asked, "Mizz Tubman, I heard you always carried a pistol with you. Would you kill a reluctant escapee that was on one of your treks?"

"Yes, if he was weak enough to give out, he'd be weak enough to betray us all, and all who have helped us, and you think I'd let so many die for just one coward?"

"Can I ask, Harriet," another person spoke up, "who did you trust in the South to help you?"

"On many rescue missions, my last stop would be in Wilmington, Delaware. It was a city right on the Mason-Dixon Line. It was the home of a Quaker. He is now one of my closest friends. When I arrived at his safehouse for the first time, he hid me inside a false wall in his shop. He gave me my first pair of shoes. Quakers is almost as good as colored. They call themselves— Friends, and you can trust them every time. Sometimes they'd hide dry socks and hardtack biscuits in the holes in trees along the route for passengers."

"So, Harriet," an older woman asked, "How were you able to find the slaves that you would bring north?"

"The slaves on plantations cannot be seen talking together, so when I was in the South, gathering slaves, I sang familiar hymns singing of the heavenly journey to the land of Canaan. Those songs did not attract the attention of the masters, but they did let the brothers and sisters in bondage know something more than met the ear."

Another hand went up. "Can you tell us how much your trips south cost?"

"Well," Harriet said, "to go south and rescue folks, I had to have money and supplies. I worked half a year as a cook, seamstress, and maid in hotels, saving up my earnings. I would go south in winter when the nights are long and people are indoors. When I was ready, I would slip down the eastern shore of Delaware into Maryland and make contact with slaves that were ready to escape.

"Also, whenever I journeyed south, I needed to pay for transportation on trains and boats, plus carry food and supplies. One time I had to hide my passengers in a mound of manure. We used straws to breathe with till the slave catchers passed. Another close call happened when the patrollers were close behind us near a train station. I put my passengers on a south bound train. The trick worked because they were looking for slaves going north."

Harriet paused and said, "I have another story for you that I think you would like to hear. One time I received news that my father was going to be arrested and would be put on trial for helping a fellow slave escape. This was a serious crime in the South. Even though my father was 70 years old, he would be punished severely if he was found guilty. I made plans to head south immediately but needed money for the trip. I went to the anti-slavery society in New York City and asked for 20 dollars. I refused to leave till I got it."

An official there asked me, "Who told you to come here for 20 dollars?"

"I answered him, 'The Lord told me, sir.' "

"Well," the official said, "I guess the Lord's mistaken this time."

"No sir." I said, "The Lord is never mistaken. Anyhow, I'm going to sit here until I get it."

Harriet continued, "There were many visitors coming and going through the office. I sat down but suffered one of my spells from my head injury and blacked out. When I woke up late in the afternoon, I found a pile of bills in my lap from office strangers adding up to 60 dollars.

"I quickly gathered my things and headed south to rescue my father. When I reached my parents' home, I found that he was to be tried the next Monday. I found an old, rickety wagon of Master Thompson and an old nag of a horse that he kept around the place. I fitted him with a beat-up straw collar, and hitched him up to a pair of old chaise wheels with a board across the axle for them to sit on. I added a board with ropes that I fastened to the axle, for my parent's to rest their feet on. My mother insisted on bringing her featherbed cover and my father's broad ax had to go too.

"So with this rickety wagon we made it north over some very dangerous roads and crossings. In a way, I just removed my father's trial to heaven's higher court and brought both my parents off to Canada. In St. Catherines my family joined the African Methodist Episcopal Church and there I managed a boarding house for newly arrived freedom seekers and helped folks find jobs."

One of the organizers of the event said, "Harriet, I've heard about a group who want to send all Negroes, free and slave, back to Africa. Have you heard of this?"

Harriet chuckled and answered with a big smile on her face. "There is a parable about a farmer who sows onions and garlic on his land, but when he found that his cow's butter is too strong and unsellable, he returned to planting clover. By then it was too late—the wind had blown the onion and garlic all over the field. So, you see, white people had to get slaves to do their hard work for them, but now that their presence didn't suit them, they wanted to pack them off to Africa. But they can't do it. We're rooted here, and they can't pull us up."

A young man in the front row asked, "Mrs. Tubman, why did you do all this hard work?"

Harriet smiled. "I did not take up the work for my own benefit but for those of my race that need help." Harriet then pointed upward with her finger and said, "I tell you it's not just me. I do believe the Lord's on a mission too.

"On another one of my journeys, there were a number of slave catchers following us. I knew that danger was coming. I asked the Lord what I must do. I heard a voice in my head say, 'Turn left.' We soon came to a stream. I was again told to 'go through it'. I said to my passengers, 'We must stop here and cross this stream.' They were afraid to cross. As we stood on the water's bank, we could see that it was wide, deep, and swift. There was no bridge and no boat, and no one could swim.

"But trusting the Lord, I went into the water and so the others followed me. The water never went above my chin. Even when we thought we would be going under, it became shallower and shallower. We found afterwards, there were posters of the escaping fugitives and the officers were forewarned of our coming. We took a different route like so many fugitives in the Bible that were saved by listening to what the Lord said to them—like He was whispering to me."

Harriet continued speaking. "On another journey south, a party of fugitives was supposed to meet me. I waited in the woods so I could conduct them north. I didn't know why at the time, but they never came. Night came on with a blinding snow storm and a brutal wind. I protected myself behind the trunk of a large tree. I stayed there all night alone while the storm raged. I said to the

Lord, 'I'm going to hold steady on to you, and I know you'll see me through.' "

In the front row, a lady's hand went up. She asked, "Harriet, didn't you almost feel when you were alone like that, that there was no God?"

Harriet answered, "Oh, no, misses, I just asked Jesus to take care of me, and he never let me get frostbitten, not one bit. I always knew I'd have help."

A man stood up at the back of the room and asked, "Harriet, weren't you afraid of the blood hounds and slave catchers?"

"Yes, I was. Another time, I felt compelled to go down for some company of slaves. I knew I was being watched everywhere. There was a meeting of slaveholders and they were determined to capture me—dead or alive. My friends begged me not to go in the face of this new danger. But I was not afraid. My answer to them was: 'John the apostle said he saw the heavenly city. He saw twelve gates. Three of those gates was in the North; three of them were in the East; and three of them were in the West, and three more gates in the South. I reckon, they might kill me down there, but I'll still get into one of them gates!' God was always near. He gave me the strength."

"I never knew a time when I did not trust Him with all abiding confidence. I talk to God as a man talks with his friend. Mine is not the religion of the morning and evening prayer at stated times, but when I feel the need, I simply trust Him to set it right. When folks were given praise, I'd say, 'Twasn't me, 'twas the Lord! I always hold to Him. I don't know where to go or what to do, but I expect you to lead me,' and He always did. The work is now well started, and I know God will take up others to care for the future. So God bless you all, and thank you for coming."

Lou, Tilly, and I saw Harriet speak those last words before a packed audience and accept a bouquet of yellow roses. All around her people knew they were witnessing a soldier of truth and gave her money for her next mission. I was a witness to the many things she did for others, often risking her own life.

Like Moses who led the Israelite slaves through the Red Sea, Harriet parted the cotton fields of many southern plantations and led the enslaved to the Promised Land. I knew if she asked, I would follow her. I do believe Harriet, like Moses of the Old Testament, listened to the Lord and I am sure He must have whispered from on high, 'Come up higher, Harriet. Come up higher.'

Chapter 3:
Way Down South In Dixie

HARRIET DIDN'T KNOW EXACTLY HOW, but she said she always knew when there was danger near her. Her heart, she said, would go flutter, flutter. She told me one day, "Cece, they may say, '*Peace, Peace*,' as much as they like, but I know there is gonna be war!"

In 1860 the first shot was fired at Fort Sumter. The War of the Rebellion had begun. Union army commanders sent out a call for teachers and nurses. Hundreds of Northerners answered the cry, including Harriet. Massachusetts Governor John Andrew sent for Harriet. He was aware of Harriet's Underground Railroad efforts and her passion to help the abolitionists. For Harriet this was an honor and the call she had been waiting for.

"Harriet," he said, "would you be willing to act as a spy and scout for the Union army and if need be, to act as a hospital nurse, or give any required service for the Union cause?"

"Yes, Governor Andrew," she said, "I will, but I have to make arrangements for my elderly parents that they wouldn't be wanting for anything while I am away."

And so, at the request of the federal government, Harriet was soon to become a part of the United States Army in South Carolina. Before being transferred, Harriet returned to Auburn to make preparations for the care and support of her parents and others living in her home. She also brought a little girl named Margaret, who she said was her niece, to live at William H. Seward's home.

Now some friendships just happen, and Harriet took a liking to Lou, Tilly, and me. We both came from Maryland's slave plantations. I was about ten or so years younger than Harriet. But more importantly, we had the same sense of what needed to be done next. So when Harriet asked Tilly and me to travel south and join up with the Union Army as a nurse and cook, we knew we had to go.

Harriet said, "We will be going south to help the contrabands. I have to report to Surgeon Henry Durant at the contraband hospital in Beaufort."

"Contrabands?" asked Tilly. "Harriet, that sounds like some kind of medicine. What are contrabands?"

"About a year ago," Harriet said, "the Union navy and army liberated the Sea Islands off the coast of South Carolina and their main harbor of Port Royal. The white planter families left their plantations for the mainland, leaving behind over 10,000 of their slaves. General Butler and the Union army is calling them folks contrabands. They are no longer considered slaves, but they are not legally free either. Most of them are destitute, with barely any clothes on their backs. We're going to teach those homeless people how to care for themselves, and I will be working to find jobs for the healthy ones. The Union army is flooded with them."

In March 1862, we were sent to Beaufort, South Carolina to help out. We soon heard the contrabands speaking a dialect called Gullah. We could barely understand what they were saying. Their language was made up of a lot of African words mixed in with English. Harriet said, "They laugh when they hear me talk, and I couldn't understand them no how."

The contrabands were suspicious of whites and those who worked for them including Harriet, so she said, "I am entitled to army rations, but I am giving them up. I don't want the contrabands thinking I'm better than they are. But that leaves me a bit short on funds. Cece and Tilly, I have an idea.

"My mother was a cook in the big house and she taught me all about cookin'. After escaping to the North, I was hired as a cook in Pennsylvania and New Jersey. I think I could make up for the loss of rations by making money on the side by setting up an eating-house in Beaufort. After my day's work I will be making root beer, pies, and gingerbread, and selling them to the troops. I've been asking some of the cooks if they might be able to help me out. Do you think you ladies would be willing to volunteer?"

"Yes, Harriet, we will," Tilly and I said. "Even though our day job is exhausting, we can help."

So during the day we cared for the sick and needy, and several nights a week we often gathered with other cooks in Harriet's cabin. Over a hot stove, we made berry pies, great quantities of gingerbread, and barrels of root beer. She got a few contrabands to sell them for her in the camps. Soldiers loved a little taste of home. I watched Harriet as she worked and thought to myself that this woman everyone is calling Moses, is supplying manna from heaven to the Union army.

The sick and wounded soldiers poured into Beaufort. The hospitals were filled with soldiers with ghastly wounds. The suffering troubled us. Daily, as nurses we bathed and cleaned soldiers' wounds. I said to Harriet, "Every day I go to the hospital and get big chunks of ice and put them into a basin and fill it with water. By the time I bathe three or four soldiers, the heat melts the ice and the water is blood-red."

"I know, Cece. The first man I come to, I thrash away the flies, and they rise like bees around a hive. When I go get more ice and get back to the next one, the flies are running around the first one black and thick as ever."

Harriet continued, "So many of these soldiers are dying. It's our duty to make them as comfortable as possible. But they tell me now, I got to report to a hospital in Florida. I asked the commanders if you and Tilly could go too. Is that all right with you?"

"Sure," I said. "I know Tilly would like to go. She is always up for traveling. I heard the soldiers down there already have one foot in the grave from that awful disease called dysentery. I also heard they have more pain-in-the-neck flies and heat there, than we got here."

"Well, I got a remedy for that stinky disease, if the army will let me try," chuckled Harriet. "My daddy, Ben Ross, taught me survival skills. My mother taught me about herbs and healing roots. I think we could cure the sickness if we could find the same roots and herbs that grew in Maryland. We're going to save those boys with some old-fashioned folk remedies. Lord willing, that will do the trick."

So in Florida, the three of us went off searching the swamps and woods till we found water lilies and a kind of geranium called crane's bill. We boiled the roots and herbs and made a bitter-tasting brew that we gave to a man who was dying—and it worked. After a day or two, he was back on duty. So Harriet boiled up a pot of those roots and herbs. General David Hunter told us to take two cans around and give it to anyone in camp that needed it.

Harriet, Tilly and I never got any bad diseases. She said the Lord would take care of us, and He did. Everyone was saying no one would die if Moses was at their bedside.

In December of 1862, we transferred back to Beaufort. It seems the war in the South was heating up. President Lincoln must have known and stacked the ranks along the coasts of South Carolina with commanding officers who were self-declared abolitionists. It was a war with powerful officers who were not to be trifled with like Major General David Hunter, General Rufus Saxton, Colonel Thomas Higginson, and Colonel James Montgomery.

Harriet said, "I know we got fierce fighting men but God won't let Master Lincoln beat the South until he does the right thing. Master Lincoln, he's a great man, and I am a poor Negro, but this Negro can tell Master Lincoln how to save money and young men. He can do it by setting the Negroes free."

Once on Hilton Head, Harriet performed the duty of a Union spy and leader of army scouts. She said, "General Hunter needs information about Confederate troop movements, encampments, and supplies. I'll be going up and down rivers and into swamps to find enemy positions and fortifications beyond the Union pickets.

"I'll be sending my so called black dispatches directly to General Hunter. Also, I've recruited a nine-man spy unit of black riverboat pilots who know the local waterways to scout for the Union. I want them to map the Sea Islands and shores of South Carolina. I'll be teaching them how to gather intelligence."

"Harriet," Tilly said, "I know with your experience on the Underground Railroad that those soldiers will be learning from a master conductor and spy. With all your disguises, you are the army's best secret agent."

"Thank you, Tilly. But I know the real reason why me and other Negroes are effective as spies down here. It's because the white Confederates think we haven't any intelligence to do so. We're like invisible people to them. They don't pay us any attention.

"In addition to all this scouting and spying, I've made it my business to see all the contrabands escaping from the plantations. I get more intelligence information from them than anybody else. Also, I received from the office of William Seward, $100 in Secret Service funds to pay those who give good information about the location of the rebel troops and weapons. Word is out about the reward money. The contrabands come see me all by their selves 'cause they've been told, '*Go see Miss Harriet. She pays good money for good information.*' "

To me, Harriet never really looked worried, but she loved to sing and hummed her favorite gospel hymns when there was something important on her mind. One afternoon, when Tilly and I were helping Harriet mend soldiers' uniforms, Harriet began a stream of low humming of 'Go Down Moses' and 'Bound for the Promised Land'.

Quietly she said, "I've been asked by General Hunter to lead an expedition along with Colonel Montgomery of three gunboats north up the Combahee River. We have been ordered to destroy Confederate supplies, take out railroads and bridges, and disable the mines that have been placed in the river by the Rebs."

Harriet went on, "I now know the whereabouts of the slaves that placed those torpedoes in the river. I'm going up the river on a reconnaissance mission tonight with my scouts to capture those men. I'm going to trade them their freedom for information about the location of those torpedoes."

"But Harriet," I said, "when you're spying out there in Confederate territory, you are considered by the Rebs to be a fugitive slave. You won't live very long if you get caught."

"I know, Cece, but I can't give up on what I'm bound to do. I got to get ready now and meet up with my scouts." Harriet gave us a little pat on the shoulder and left in a hurry. I stayed up all night praying for her safety. Pacing the floor and drinking cups of black coffee was all I could do to settle my jangling nerves.

When I saw Harriet the next morning, she looked tired and smelled of mud and swamp grass. I said, "Lordy, Lordy, I'm glad to see you back. Did you find those snitches? Did they tell you where those bad torpedoes are in the water?"

"Yes, they did," Harriet said, "and tomorrow we're going upstream with 150 soldiers of Colonel Montgomery's 2nd South Carolina black troops and go deep into Confederate territory. This is the first time that I have been asked to lead a major Union military operation. We're taking three gunboats up the Combahee River."

"But Harriet," Tilly said, "you said the river has torpedoes in the water. What are they?"

"Well, the military calls them torpedoes, but they're floating mines, full of explosives, in the water that can blow a ship up if you hit them."

"So," I said, "hitting just one of them mines could kill everybody, including you?"

"Yes, but I now know the location of the all the mines. I know too where slaves are waiting for us to bring them off to freedom. We are planning on raiding three estates of prominent secessionists. They are going to get their comeuppance from the same slaves that are now soldiers on this mission. The burning will soon begin."

Early in the morning on June 2nd, Harriet, Colonel Montgomery, and 150 black soldiers boarded the gunboats. Later I heard what happened. They told me Harriet would lean way overboard peering into the dark water pointing and directing the ship's captain to move right or left in the channel. Harriet steered the ships with the skilled precision of a trained, veteran of explosives.

At first light, Colonel Montgomery ordered his troops onshore, close to the targeted estates. He turned and shouted to Harriet, "Take care, *General* Tubman, and let those southerners be made to feel that this is a real war."

Gunfire from the surrounding woods soon erupted. Shots were fired, but the attackers were quickly overwhelmed. The frightened plantation slaves saw the gunboats and the gunfire and ran into the woods like startled deer. But by some mysterious messaging, the word went out that these were 'Lincoln's gunboats' come to set them free.

On hearing the ship's whistle, the plantation slaves then ran down every road, and across every field, and crowded onto the riverbanks, over 700 of them. Harriet and Montgomery's troops began burning the plantation buildings to the ground. More shots were fired but the raiding party returned unharmed to the landing. The contrabands in the water, fearing they would be left behind, hung onto the small boats that would ferry them to the large gunboats. The oarsmen tried beating their hands, but they would not let go.

Colonel Montgomery shouted from the upper deck to Harriet,

"Moses, you'll have to give them a song. Sing to them Harriet— quick. We got to push off."

So Harriet began singing hymns in her beautiful voice:

"Of all the whole creation in the East and in the West,
The glorious Yankee nation is the greatest and the best.
Come along! Come along! Don't be alarmed,
Uncle Sam is rich enough to give you all a farm."

At the end of every verse, them poor folks in their enthusiasm clapped their hands over their heads and shouted, "Glory, glory." With that, the oarsmen started rowing and when all were on board the gunboats, they were able to get moving back down the river.

Upon arriving back at Port Royal, the party received a warm welcome. This victory was a great morale boost to the Union since it hadn't yet had a decisive win in the North in months.

Harriet said, "I heard tell we carried away 727 of the Confederacy's so-called property. We marched right into their neighborhood with very little resistance and burned that whole section of county without the loss of a single life. The bullets were whizzing past me, but all I suffered was a torn skirt. It seems like the Rebs were asleep. It reminded me of all the children of Israel coming out of Egypt."

"Land sakes, I'm just glad you're back in one piece, Harriet," I said. "A torn skirt can be easily mended, but soon you got to order one of those new bloomer dresses. Then you won't be tripping on your long skirts and can make a fast run when you need too. But I bet the Reb will be groaning, when they hear that the raid was led by a woman, let alone a black woman. I do believe you are the only woman who has led soldiers into battle during this war."

"Yes, Cece. That's true, but also this mission is a real blow to the Confederate cause. During the raid, Colonel Montgomery called me by the name of *General* Tubman. He knows that's what

John Brown used to call me. But I hear there's a big battle coming up in Charleston, and that won't be an easy fight."

Back in camp, we heard about the ship and troop movements out of Hilton Head and Beaufort. We knew a mighty conflict was about to begin and that nurses would soon be ordered to the Union base camp close to Fort Sumter.

The Union blue was everywhere. But Harriet and I knew that soon things would be covered in dark, red blood.

Chapter 4:
Climbing Jacob's Ladder

I N January of 1863, the word went out throughout the North about forming an all-black regiment. Lincoln needed more troops. The battles in 1862: in April of Shiloh with 13,000 casualties, in August the Second Battle of Bull Run with 14,000, Antietam in September with 23,000, and Fredericksburg in December with 12,000 casualties, was staggering. The Union troops were bloody and weary. By the end of 1862 the flood of volunteers slowed down to a trickle. In the cook's kitchen, I kneaded bread with the same fury that troops displayed on the battlefield. In February, 1863, the army mail carrier delivered a letter from my brother. He wrote,

"Dear Cece,

Frederick Douglass has been a hero of mine ever since Harriet brought us to his home when we were fugitives on the Underground Railroad. I knew he and Governor Andrew of Massachusetts were looking for black men to enlist in the Union army. I heard Douglass was giving a speech close by, so I decided to go and hear him.

At the gathering, Douglass said that the 54th Massachusetts Volunteers was the first free black regiment authorized by Congress to fight for the Union. He shouted to the crowd, 'To me the idea of fighting the South without using black soldiers is like fighting with one arm tied behind your back. Let us win for ourselves the gratitude of our country, and the best blessings of our posterity through all time. Men of color, to arms!"

"Right then, Cece, I decided to enlist. Frederick Douglass' two sons, Lewis and Charles, were the first black men from New York State to join the 54th Massachusetts. I believe this is a way to show the nation that the black man can fight. We want Lincoln to know that we're not cowards. I am ready to enter the battle and die for the cause.

I'm now part of the 54th and proud to be with these soldiers. It's all because of the one sentence in Lincoln's Emancipation Proclamation that said, 'black men could now be received into the armed services of the United States'. Because of that, Massachusetts Governor Andrew fought for and won the right to raise the first black regiment in the North. He insisted on strict requirements for all enlisters. Many men were turned down because they couldn't pass the medical exam which was harder than exams given to white solders. The doctor in charge kept saying, 'We want only perfect men, physically and mentally ready for combat.'

"By Governor Andrew's order, most men who enlisted have been born free and never knew the lash or called anyone master. Most can read and write. There is a doctor, a druggist, and engineers and printers among us. Massachusetts couldn't supply all the men needed to fill up the ranks so, Governor Andrew sent out recruiters like Frederick Douglass to Connecticut, New York, Pennsylvania, Missouri, and even Canada. There was a lot of pressure on men in black communities by their fathers, sisters, and sweethearts to go forward and fight. The ranks filled up fast. When the 1,000-man quota was reached, the recruiting stations closed their doors.

The regiment's officers were chosen, but Governor Andrew was angry with the War Department's decision about the regiment's commanders. They said that the commissioned officers from lieutenant to colonel had to be white. The corporals and sergeants could be black. Governor Andrew picked Robert Gould Shaw to lead the 54th. I've been told he is 25 years old and is the son of an abolitionist. For the last two years,

Shaw had been a captain the in the 2nd Massachusetts Volunteers. He has seen a lot of action and fought and was wounded at Antietam. So we are now becoming a fighting unit.

All enlistees are being sent by train to Camp Meigs in Readville, Massachusetts. When I am settled there, I will write again. I have enclosed some newspaper clipping that you, Harriet, and Tilly might like to see. —Your loving brother, Lou."

———————— ·••· ————————

With that Lou enlisted. My heart shuddered to think what might be his fate. I had already seen too much pain and death, but I knew Lou was right. There was only one way to stop the wild beast called War.

I told Harriet and Tilly about the news from my brother and showed them the newspaper clippings. I said, "It looks like Lou has underlined some spots in these articles. Here's something he highlighted. It's a quote from Frederick Douglass, 'Once let the black man get upon his person the brass letters US on his buckle, let him get an eagle on his button, the musket on his shoulder, and bullets in his pocket and there will be no power on earth that can deny him citizenship to the United States.'

This one too is underlined. 'The best way to win the war is to let the black man fight. The day dawns; the morning star is bright on the horizon. The iron gate of our imprisonment is half way open. One gallant rush from our northern brothers will fling it wide open and four million of our brothers and sisters will march into liberty.'

"Look, Lou wrote across the page, *Slavery is doomed!*"

"Lou's right, Cece," Harriet said. "These soldiers will change the face of war. For years the black abolitionists and ministers have preached this from the pulpit. Master Lincoln has ignored far too long the strong arm of the black man to help. The idea of black troops with weapons has been the southern man's worst nightmare.

There has always been the fear of slaves rising up against their masters. Black people have, for far too long been abused and kept in chains. So now being given weapons and a chance to get even, why wouldn't they?"

"You're right, Harriet," Tilly said. "Black soldiers are going to rally around the flag and save the war and their race."

I didn't hear from Lou for a while, but I heard reports from Harriet about their training. Finally another letter came in June.

"Dear Cece,

Hope all is going well for you. My training consists of breakfast, drill, lunch drill, dinner drill and more drill. I've learned there are at least nine separate commands for loading and firing a weapon. We are striving for perfection. Many of us have even gone out to watch the white troops as they trained here at camp to learn more.

At times crowds of local people and dignitaries come to watch us drill. They are looking for any sign of unwillingness, inability or inferiority. I think in the beginning, we were the most laughed at, cursed, and despised unit in the army. But now as more people have seen us up close that has changed. I heard Governor Andrew said, 'This regiment will be the vanguard, the noble experiment, and it must not fail.' For all of us, the weight of our race is heavy upon us.

It's been about 100 days, since we arrived at Camp Meigs. I've heard we will be sailing soon for South Carolina but I don't know where. Colonel Shaw told us 'We will leave this state with as good as a regiment, which ever marched.' We been told there are plans for a huge farewell parade for us in downtown Boston. I hope this letter reaches you. As soon as I know where we are headed, I will try and let you know. —-Love Lou"

Very early one morning I heard an urgent knock at the door. It was Tilly. I opened it and she said, "Cece, it's me. Get up quick. The 54th is here in Beaufort right now. They're all on a big ship in the harbor and they are about to disembark. Hurry! Let's go and see them."

Tilly and I ran quickly down to the waterfront where a small crowd was gathering. Sure enough, the men were already stepping onto the shore. The sun was just coming up and in the pre-dawn light, it was hard to see the soldiers marching past us. More transports brought a continuous stream of soldiers. I couldn't wait to see if Lou was there.

It was Tilly who saw him first. In the double line of soldiers filing past, Lou was nearest to me. I couldn't help but yell, "Lou, it's me, Cece."

Lou looked over and gave a quick nod but marched steadily on. I was so excited and proud. I squeezed Tilly's hand and cried a bit. She said, "Let's ask Harriet where they are going. She might know."

As we turned around to leave, there was a soldier on a white horse striding past wearing the eagle's insignia on his shoulders. An older gentleman next to us gasped. "That's Colonel Shaw. He looks young, but he has the face of a man who has seen many battles."

Tilly and I jumped up and down in excitement. After the 54th set up camp, Lou came to see me at the bakery. It was one of those times that we just couldn't stop hugging. I was proud of him in his new blue uniform and shiny buttons.

"I didn't expect that you would be stationed here in Beaufort, Lou," I said.

"I don't know if I will be for long. You see we are camped about five miles from here at a plantation that is on top of a swampy bog. There are mosquitoes out there that could carry a horse away. If someone asked me what I saw of the South, it would be stinkweed, rattlesnakes and alligators.

When we arrived at the camp site, there were very little supplies. Colonel Shaw was really angry about it. I heard he's going to contact Governor Andrew. We are still under Governor Andrew's command because we haven't been officially sworn in under federal law. It's just awful out there.

"But Colonel Shaw is doing what's right by us. He fought for shoes when two-thirds of the men had none. He's been fighting for uniforms, rifles, and equal pay for us, when most think it's a bad idea because everyone believes that we were hired as laborers, not as fighting men. But Colonel Shaw is determined to prove them wrong.

"And that ain't all, Cece. Once we were on the payroll, they decided in Washington, to pay us just ten dollars a month, not the regular white man's pay of thirteen, plus take out three dollars for our uniforms. Colonel Shaw said, 'You are risking your lives the same as any white man and you should get paid the same. A black man's life is worth the same as a white man's. All men die equal.'

"So, we voted and all of us including Colonel Shaw and his officers, decided to serve without any wages till the government pays us the same as and any other Union soldier. It's an honor to belong to the 54th, not just because it's a black regiment, but because Colonel Shaw is its commander."

"But I heard, Lou that people are saying that a black regiment will run at the first shot fired."

"I know what they are saying, Cece, that we haven't seen the white elephant yet, right?"

"What are you talking about, Lou? You crazy? There are no elephants around these parts, let alone white ones."

"It's soldier talk. It means we haven't been in battle and been under enemy fire. But we've got a chance to be men of honor for all black people. I keep hearing in my head the words that Frederick Douglass said the day we left Boston. He said, 'Once you have spent your blood, no man again will ever be enslaved. Smash the chains of slavery.' We will, Cece, we going to smash those chains."

"I know you will, Lou. You are one of the strongest and bravest people I know. I just want you to be careful." Lou and I sat and talked for a long time, drinking coffee, eating pie, and telling stories. Before long, it was time for him to go.

"Cece, I'd like to take a piece of your pie and some cornbread back to camp with me."

"Sure enough. You can take a whole pie with you and lots of cornbread."

"I know some men that would really enjoy that. Thanks, Sis."

"You come back soon. Harriet would like to see you again too."

"I will. You say hello to her for me. I'll come back as soon as I can. I have met a lot of new friends and I would like you to meet some. How's that sound?"

"Sure, Lou." As he left, I could see that Lou was not the boy that escaped with Harriet on the Underground Railroad. He was a soldier of the 54th and the nation.

Chapter 5:
Wishing

P ERMANENT HAPPINESS WAS NEVER SOMETHING I thought would come to me. I had seen too much of plantation life and war. But it is curious how there are sometimes hints there may be small shifts in one's life.

My mother told me when I was a little girl, if a ladybug landed on your finger, to let it alone and make a wish when it flew away. I was sitting outside the nurse's quarters late one afternoon and a beautiful little ladybug was near me in the grass. The minute I put down a leaf next to her, she came running toward my hand and then onto my finger.

I believed she looked right at me and after a long moment, she flew away. I quickly made a wish. Then suddenly it felt like something broke inside of me. Tears ran down my face and I sobbed and sobbed. Harriet and Tilly were doing laundry around the corner and they came running.

"Cece, what's wrong?" Harriet asked. "What's happened? Has there been another skirmish?"

"No, Harriet. It's me. I'm tired and my mind is worn out by seeing so many wounded soldiers. I see death all around me every day and I am feeling older and older. I feel sad and lonely when solders talk to me about their wives and sweethearts back home. I've been wishing for a long time for a beau of my own. I feel so guilty for even thinking like this, when there is terrible pain on so many faces. I don't see any future for me. I'm sorry for carrying on like this. I just yearn for someone special, in my own life."

Harriet smiled at me like a mother would look at a small child and said. "Cece, you been so brave and been working way beyond what the good Lord asks of you or any soldier around here. You need to be kinder to yourself and don't you go getting sorrowful about getting older. You're still young. When it's time, there will be someone for you—sometime when you least expect it."

"But Harriet, I been praying now for a long time. I even found those silly ladybugs that my mama told me to make wishes on all around me. One just now came crawling right up to me and sat on my finger. Yesterday when I went to bed there was a couple on my blanket, and some settled on my clothes. Those ladybugs are finding and following me everywhere. I am so wished-out and feel so guilty for even asking for something when so many are sacrificing their very lives. I am ashamed of myself, but I can't stop feeling sad inside."

"Cece, stop. You have a right to your feelings. I once felt the same as you do now. I worked hard on the plantation and watched all the young girls find beaus. Then one night I met John Tubman. John was about thirty-two years and was born to free parents. Because he was a free born man, he moved about the county working for different farmers and owners as a laborer. He lived and worked in the Peter's Neck area, south of Tobacco Stick near where my father worked.

"I met John Tubman at one of the social events that happened during harvest time. We danced and carried on like young children. It wasn't long after that, that we jumped the broom and settled into married life. I loved John Tubman with all my heart, but he was free and I was not. I talked to him about my secret plan to run away north to freedom, but he would have no part of it. He warned me that if I tried to run away, he would warn the owner Eliza Brodess.

"When I heard I was about to be sold south, I made a plan

to escape with my brothers. But after a short run for it, they were scared and they talked me into turning back. My husband never knew I had tried to run away that night. I just crept back to our cabin and laid quietly at his side. The second try, I made it north, but I never forgot about John.

"I decided in 1851 to go back along the Underground Railroad and bring him north with me. But when I arrived in Dorchester County, I heard that John had taken another wife, a free woman named Caroline. Instead of me making a scene, I sent word to John that I was hiding close by with friends and that I wanted to take him north. He refused and he sent word that he had moved on and would continue to live in Dorchester County. He didn't have any ambition about leaving the South. He was more than comfortable living the way he was.

"At first I was determined to go and make all the trouble I could, not caring if the master caught me. I was overwhelmed with anger and hurt for the lost dream of a free future with my husband. But I quickly realized that it was foolish to make mischief. I said to myself, 'If he could do without me, then I could do without him. I right then, dropped him out of my heart.' I decided not to waste an opportunity, and so I gathered a group of slaves and brought them north with me to Philadelphia."

"Oh, Harriet, I didn't know that about your husband."

"It's hard to make any sense of it, honey. I don't mean to say that all men are the same. Your brother and the men of the 54th Massachusetts Volunteers are good strong men and by my thinking the bravest of the brave. Those ladybugs you've been seeing are messengers of promise. They bring word that you can leave your worries behind you and happiness is on the way. Cece, let go of your fears, have faith. Let romance find you."

"So it is not just coincidence about all those ladybugs?"

"No, you already know the answer to that. It's trust."

The three of us went back to doing laundry and spent the night making cornbread and berry pies. Harriet always had the mind of an entrepreneur. A few of Harriet's contraband friends picked up our baked goods in the morning and loaded them into their baskets to sell around the camp. Harriet also rented a small store in Beaufort for selling her wares and took laundry and sewing in from the soldiers.

I never asked Harriet and maybe I didn't want to know, if she was a matchmaker or maybe the ladybugs were. But soon after I talked to her about my wanting a beau, a soldier from the 54th came into her little shop on a day when I was helping out.

The front door opened and suddenly right in front of me stood a sergeant from the 54th Volunteers. He was over six feet tall. He had a fine face and serene eyes. His face was framed by a neatly cut beard. His mouth was grave and firm with plenty of lines of courage that etched his expression. He had a clear, straightforward glance. Sometimes there's no telling what providence has in store for you. I felt goosebumps all over.

"Can I help you, sir?" I asked. "Harriet's not here right now but we have lots of pies, cornbread, and root beer. If you want, have a seat. I can bring you a cup of coffee from the back."

"So kind of you. If you don't mind, I'd like a piece of your raspberry pie. My name is Sergeant William Mellon. I am with the 54th. My friends call me Will."

"My name is Cece. That's short for Cecelia. I have a brother in the 54th. His name is Louis. He's in Company C and we're both from Dorchester County, Maryland."

"I am in Company D and I was from Maryland too, so I guess that makes us friends already."

"I guess it does, especially because we all came from the same place, including Harriet."

"I've heard about Harriet Tubman. She's a legend. I would so like to meet her."

The sergeant sat down to have his pie and coffee. Now and then, he would look over at me. All I could think of is that I wished

I had combed my hair better and put on a cleaner apron. The sergeant handed me the money for the pie and he asked, "Do you work in here every day? I might like to come back and try some of your cornbread."

"Well sir, yes, I do some times, Sergeant Mellon."

"Then I'll see you soon, and the name is Will." The sergeant walked out, and I think my heart almost stopped beating. All I could think of was his name—Sergeant William Mellon. I was not paying any attention to the pie crust I was kneading when Harriet walked in.

"Hey, Cece, I just saw a sergeant from the 54th down the way. Did he come in here?"

"Why yes, he did. I can't help say I think he was very kind and handsome. He said he would be back. If it's all right with you, I would like to be here then."

With a wink of her eye, Harriet said, "I think that is a good idea, Cece. So glad those ladybugs helped out."

After that first meeting, it was only the beginning of daily visits between Sergeant Mellon and me. We took walks, talked for hours, and soon began to hold each other's hands. There seemed to be a special sweetness when he looked at me and I felt in my heart a certain understanding that William Mellon was someone very special in my life.

One moonlit night we strolled along the Beaufort Harbor where hundreds of transports and ships were moored. The wind gently blew across the bay. The fleecy clouds soon gave way to great billowing ones. The moon softly drifted behind them. We stopped to rest for a while.

Will turned to me and said, "I know this may sound silly and a little too soon, but I have special feelings for you. I remember everything about that day I first met you—-from the flour on your hands and face to the color of your apron. I thought that you were someone I wanted to be with again and again."

I squeezed his hand and said, "I want to say my life is so much better ever since I met you. My brother has spoken very highly of you and knows of your bravery and good nature. Before you say anymore, I want you to ask if you are not feeling this way because of the urgency of war to say such things."

"I hope in time and I pray, Cece, that if I am allowed to live through this war, to make you happy and keep all harm far from you. The world will go on with its terrors, but I care about you and I am falling in love with you."

"Then I will tell you how sweet and good it is to be with you. I have thought of you in the long black nights. You may think me foolish too for saying this so quickly, but I want to say that I am not just fond of you, I am falling in love with you too. Just seeing you walking toward me makes me think I am seeing a miracle from God."

William and I kissed and said good-night. It was a night of dreams and imaginings. But we both knew that these special nights would not last long.

Chapter 6:
Harriet And The Colonel

S OMETIMES COOKS CAN SMELL TROUBLE a long way off. Each morning the ovens would heat up as we made the soldiers' bread. Rumors would fly everywhere like the flour dust that sifted in the pans.

"Did you hear the Union Army is planning to take Fort Wagner?"

"I've heard the fort is reinforced with over 100 cannons. There are even rumors that Shaw's 54th Massachusetts Volunteers will be leading the charge."

After arriving in Beaufort, Colonel Shaw and his staff set off to find out if there was a better place for the 54th to camp. We heard Shaw came back in a rage. He discovered that the white troops were stationed in an excellent location. Only the 54th and the other US Colored Troops had been sent out to camp on top of a mosquito-ridden bog with very few supplies.

Shaw immediately sent a wire to Governor Andrew who threatened to recall the 54th if the situation wasn't corrected at once. The Secretary of War didn't want to lose the 54th, so new orders were issued. It seems the quartermaster had withheld supplies deliberately as a way of degrading and demeaning the black troops. Shaw received new orders and the 54th was sent to St Simeon Island. There they were sworn in under federal service.

My whirlwind romance had been put on hold and limited to letter writing. By the end of June, Harriet and I were ordered to the

Union base camp close to Fort Sumter. The army and navy including the 54th, were gathering there and we knew what was coming. We heard there was about to be a major battle of the war with over 10,000 Union troops and 16 ironclads. Those new ironclads were the pride of navy's and were covered with metal plates, protecting them from explosives.

I was working preparing surgical supplies in one of the countless medical tents when I felt a hand on my shoulder. It was Will. I was shocked to see him on such a pre-battle day.

"Cece, I am so grateful and happy to see you. I asked where you might be and I was lucky to find you. I don't have much time. I only made it here because I have to deliver these papers to headquarters. Your brother said to tell you he loves you and he is okay with whatever happens tomorrow."

"What do you mean?" I asked.

"Tomorrow they're sending us to James Island, south of Charleston. It looks like we might see action soon. But the real target is Fort Wagner. It sits out at the entrance to the bay guarding the city of Charleston. We got to take that fort first before we can put an end to Charleston. That fort is massive and it covers the whole northern tip of Morris Island. There's no way around it.

"What I wanted to say and wished there was more time to say this is, I truly love you, Cece. I do want to spend my life with you. Please let me know if you can be with me always or if you decide not to, then I will have to learn if I can live without you."

"Please don't worry, I never stopped being yours."

"Then there is only one more word to say. It is a simple word, but a very important word. It's the word, "Yes". Will then got down on his knee and asked, "Will you marry me Cece?"

"Oh Will, I can say with all my heart, Yes."

"I know now I have found the woman I am destined to be with, I hope, forever."

"Cece, I do want to jump the broom with you. I know that there is a minister named Reverend Charles Smith in the 54th who is one of Harriet's friends. He said he would be willing to help us. Do you want to do this now?"

"Yes, of course, I do."

"Then I will see if it is possible. I love you, Cece. I will get word to you."

In a moment he was gone and I stood awestruck by the fury of love and the terror of timing.

Miracles sometimes happen. Reverend Smith, Harriet, Lou, Tilly, and Will and I were able to get a two hour leave. Tilly found violets for my bouquet and the simple words with my betrothed "I do" were spoken. Harriet added, "I think those ladybugs did you proud."

On July 11, 1863, the 54th had their first taste of battle at James Island, just west of Fort Wagner. The 54th covered the retreat of the Union troops and smashed the Rebel charge. They stood their ground before the enormous white elephant. All knew Fort Wagner was next.

Now some things might seem like just a coincidence, but I never thought so afterwards. *Harriet cooked Colonel Robert Gould Shaw's last meal.* After the colonel's officers were fed and left the room, the young colonel sat at the table talking to Harriet. I was shocked by Harriet's boldness in talking to such an important commander, but I quickly made up my mind to listen by the kitchen door.

I heard Harriet ask, "Considering tomorrow, what are you most afraid of Colonel Shaw?"

The Colonel bit his lip and answered, "That I might be wrong. I've worked hard to train the men, but will they be ready under the most dreaded conditions? By my command, I know many of them will meet their end tomorrow and go to an early grave."

"Colonel Shaw," Harriet said. "When I was leading slaves along the Underground Railroad, sometimes there was a bend in the road—a possible circling back. Tomorrow your men know that there will be no bend in the road—only a fork. Some of your troops will take the high road to heaven and others will go straight across the rampart to fight again. They know it. It doesn't make it any easier, but this is the path they have chosen."

Harriet continued, "You never know how strong you are until being strong is the only choice you've got left. That's what tomorrow brings. Your men respect you. They know what each bullet means. The 54th will show their worth to the nation."

I saw Harriet lean back in her chair, pause, and ask, "So Colonel Shaw, what is it that you want most?"

The Colonel clasped his hands like he was praying. In a deliberate voice he said, "Like most men, I want peace. There has to be a way for us to stop this bloody war."

"Colonel," Harriet said, "I hope you liked the stew that you and your officers just enjoyed. I want to say that all those stew's spices and ingredients takes time to simmer into that tasty meal that you and your men just had. I do believe, the same is true of this war. It will take time to change the hearts and minds of the North and the South, and blend and melt them together again. At this time, you are a servant at the table called history. You are the blue-eyed child of destiny, and I know you will complete the task for the greater good."

Harriet continued, "Colonel Shaw, see the vase of magnolia flowers on the table? I picked them special. They say that the magnolias were one of the first flowering plants on the earth. They will probably be here long after man is gone. Like the magnolias, I pray that you survive tomorrow's battle at Fort Wagner."

Through the crack in the kitchen door, I could see the colonel was getting ready to leave. He said he had to review his plans. I didn't understand everything that was said but it made me real scared for my brother and Will.

Before we left the kitchen, Harriet took most of the petals from the magnolia flowers and put them in her apron pocket. I know why. She was going to look for the Colonel tomorrow. The flowers were her hope to find him, alive. After Harriet left the room, I took some petals and put them in my pocket, too. I would be looking for my husband and my brother.

We didn't cook much on the day of the battle. We readied the hospitals and prepared hundreds of bandages. Before dusk we went out to watch the battle with a news reporter. We were on top of a hill overlooking the beach where the troops were gathering below. The 54th Massachusetts were lined up in strict regimental file.

Colonel Shaw dismounted. He faced his men and shouted, "We are now stepping into history." He then turned and shouted,

"Fix bayonets.

Forward men.

Quick step!"

The regiment had to funnel between the ocean and a marsh through a narrow strip of sand. They could only send one regiment rushing forward at a time. Everyone knew the causalities would be extreme in the lead regiment. All guns were aimed at them from the fort's 30-foot wall. There was murderous fire.

The barrage of the cannon fire started and could be heard fifteen miles away. The storm of the battle broke. There were thunderous claps of fire, smoke, and shell. There were cries of pain everywhere. The assault went on from dusk into the black of night. The soldiers walked into the teeth of death. It was a slaughter pit.

I never saw the likes of this. I was terrified. I could not stop shaking and started screaming at the top of my lungs, "No more. No more Harriet. Where's my husband? Where's my brother?" I covered my eyes with my apron and sunk to the ground.

I heard Harriet yelling in my ear, "So sorry Cece, I know you're shocked and scared, but these men are fighting for freedom and glory. I pray for your brother, Will, and all of our brave men to be protected by all the angels in heaven tonight."

After many hours, the firing stopped and the smoke began

to lift. There was a truce. As nurses, we were ordered onto the battlefield to help with the dead and wounded. The carnage was beyond comprehension. It was a grisly scene. The dead lay in contorted positions, mangled by cannon fire.

I found my brother. He was wounded in the arm and chest. The stretcher bearers came and took him to the hospital tents. I frantically looked for my husband. I grabbed every soldier I saw and asked him if he saw Sergeant William Mellon. No one knew anything.

With so many screaming and dying men, I could barely think about what to do next. The moans of dying men could be heard, begging for help. Soldiers grabbed my skirt and pleaded with me for water. The temperature when the sun rose hovered near 90 degrees, adding the odor of dead men to the dreadful landscape.

Two soldiers with a stretcher ran past me. I begged them for help in finding Will. One said to look over by the moat that surrounded the fort. He said a lot of men over there had not been picked up yet. I ran scrambling over barb wire and dead men searching for Will. Many of the men in that area had drowned when the tide came in. So many were covered in mud and gun powder, it was hard to distinguish their faces.

I suddenly saw a man that looked in size like my Will, but I couldn't be sure. I wiped away the mud from his face and screamed, "Will, you're alive!" I ran for stretcher-bearers. Will was alive. My love was alive.

I went with Will to the nearest hospital tent. He was wounded in the back and was having a hard time breathing. The nearest head nurse said, "Try not to worry, he will be fine. You better get back to the battlefield and help the other nurses and soldiers." In obedience to orders, I began my way back to the battlefield at once. Running by the lines of wounded soldiers I heard the frightening words from dazed soldiers, "He's dead. Colonel Shaw is dead and half the regiment is shot up."

"Oh no it can't be," I thought. I saw Harriet going into headquarters. I ran fast to catch up with her.

"Harriet," I said, "things are bad out there, real bad. I found Will and Lou—they're alive."

"Good, I'm glad to hear that, but this is much worse than anyone expected. Those poor boys were cut to pieces."

"I just heard outside that Colonel Shaw is dead."

Harriet lowered her head and said in a quiet quivering voice, "I did too. I was told that he died rallying his men on the rampart of the fort. They said there were so many bullet holes in his uniform that they were hard to count."

Harriet clasped her hands over her face. She looked pale and was shaking like she did sometimes before she had her spells. I pulled her into the officer's dining room and ran to get her a cup of water. Harriet sat silent in a chair, rocking herself. She was mumbling, "Oh Lord, by all the heavens above, let those brave men and Colonel Shaw rest in peace. Let them rest in peace, Oh Lord let 'em rest in peace, rest in peace."

Harriet then got up and put the magnolia petals from her apron pocket on the chair where Colonel Shaw sat a little while before. She then turned and looked out a window at the turmoil in camp.

I saw on the dining room table a small note. It had Harriet's name on it. I asked her if she wanted to me read it. She nodded so I began.

"Dear Harriet,

I was just informed that General Lee was turned back at Gettysburg. I pray the war is turning and for strength to do my sacred duty. It is all about overcoming fear and doing what is right. If I die tomorrow, it is for the greater cause. I will remember your kind words. Tell everyone, you served me my last supper—and that it was good."

—-Colonel Robert Gould Shaw, Commander of the 54th Massachusetts Volunteers, July 18, 1863.

Chapter 7:
Saving Old Glory

FOR DAYS AFTER A BATTLE, there was ongoing death, and sorrow. All of the medical tents and hospitals around the Union encampments were filled with the wounded. Soldiers were being transported to hospitals in Beaufort and Hilton Head. All surgeons and nurses worked tirelessly without sleep or rest. The only thing that sustained us was seeing the quiet fortitude of the stricken soldiers lying before us waiting patiently and bravely for help.

My brother was in a medical tent not far from where I was stationed. Will was taken to the main hospital at Port Royal. Harriet and I asked recovering soldiers to tell us more about what happened during the battle at Fort Wagner.

Harriet heard about the courage of William Carney of the 54th, and found him in a nearby medical tent. She knew he made it across the rampart and so wanted to talk with him. She asked permission to see him for a brief visit. I went too.

Harriet began, "William Carney? My name is Harriet Tubman and this is Cece. We're nurses. I heard that during the battle, you were shot several times and that you were the soldier that planted the flag on the top of Fort Wagner. It would help to know what happened. No one is telling us much. They are all sick or sick at heart. Can you talk about it?"

Other soldiers were beginning to gather around him, curious to hear about what Carney knew. "Yes, I can," he said. "I can talk for a while, but with the pain from the bullets I took in my arm, leg, and head, I drift in and out. Mrs. Tubman, I am so glad to meet you. I am a bloody mess, but I am honored that you would come over and talk with me. You're a legend. Many men here would die for you. You're one of the heroes of this war."

Harriet reached out to touch William Carney's hand and spoke in her deep, strong voice. "Soldier, I would be much obliged if you could tell us more about the battle. I've heard over half of the 600 men that were sent into battle from the 54th regiment, are dead, missing, or wounded. Can you tell us anything about Colonel Shaw? I heard he was killed. We heard the artillery fire from the six ironclad ships out in the bay beginning at sun-up that never stopped till dusk. The smoke was so thick we did not see much."

Carney paused, sighed and began, "Yes, every hour the bombardment increased. Our camp filled with the ash. We coughed and choked on it. The noise was like a mad giant pounding on a bass drum. I heard that General Quincy Gillmore who replaced General Hunter, promised Colonel Shaw, 'There will be almost no one left alive after our guns are finished with the place.' That was not the truth."

Carney continued, "We thought we would be storming a fort that had been smashed and most of the Rebs killed. Also we didn't know right away, but the big guns inside the fort hadn't been touched. The Confederate guns must have been moved below, away from the outer walls. Fort Wagner's outside walls were made of palmetto logs and they didn't crack under the bombardment of exploding shells. Many of the shells just bounced off their fortifications."

Harriet interrupted, "I heard that Colonel Shaw volunteered the 54th to spearhead the assault."

Carney nodded and said, "Yes, he did. Colonel Shaw ordered us to rest till it was time to move forward. We waited, cleaned, and readied our rifles. Before the battle started, Colonel Shaw walked among us saying, 'The eyes of thousands will be on what you do tonight.' He also went through the ranks and looked at soldier's pictures from home, and talked freely to his troops about their wives and families.

"Before long the Union guns stopped booming and it was silent. Three red-tailed rockets hissed from the ironclads and a signal gun went off at camp's headquarters indicating the start of the assault. At 5:45 p.m. sharp the assembly was sounded and we formed ranks. My company's orders were to storm the right flank of the fort, the side nearest the ocean. We dug in on the side of a sand dune about 1,000 yards away from Fort Wagner.

"At dusk Colonel Shaw dismounted his horse and spoke. 'Men, you must prove yourselves tonight. Follow the colors.' With his sword drawn Colonel Shaw shouted,

"Forward, 54th! Forward!'

"We were all surprised by the colonel deciding to lead us into battle. I do believe it's pretty much unheard of for such a high ranking officer to do that. But Colonel Shaw with a determined look, marched us forward.

In rigid ranks, six-hundred of the 54th, followed across a three-quarter mile stretch of open beach. We attacked in two wings of five companies each. For the men on the right flank, the beach narrowed until we had to wade knee-deep in the ocean. The men on the left flank stumbled through a marsh, crisscrossed wire, and a deep moat. Smoke from the day-long shelling ringed the fort like a wreath."

Carney took a deep breath and went on, "Even though the lines were no longer perfect, we staggered on. When the front line was within 300 yards from the fort's outer works, the moon came out from behind a cloud. At 200 yards, we heard a shout from the fort's parapet, 'Open fire!'

"Suddenly, shells from the Confederate battery slammed into the earth. The enemy had seen our colors. We were hit by a barrage of canister, musketry, and shelling from the fort. Flames from the Confederate rifles hit us again. We fell in heaps—cut down by a rain of bullets. Before the Rebs had time to reload, Colonel Shaw sprang up with his sword overhead and screamed, 'Charge!'

"Hearing his voice, our regiment recovered. We ran forward. We were doubled over and low, to protect ourselves from enemy fire. Another hail of shell and bullets hit us and more men fell, devastating the 54th. Shrapnel fired from enemy cannons smashed into us. We raced on. Men all around me crumpled—dead or badly wounded. Fort Wagner became a mound of fire pouring streams of shot and shell. The outer earthworks were so steep that the Rebs were rolling cannon balls down, killing soldiers in mass. It was a dead man's hell.

"Colonel Shaw drove us forward again, yelling, 'Rally 54th! Rally!'

"The colonel made it to the top of the parapet with the flag bearer right behind him. Then I saw Colonel Shaw pitch forward off the wall into the fort. He was shot in the heart—dead. Sergeant John Wall was the color bearer but a fatal bullet struck him too. I saw him stagger and about to drop the flag.

"I dropped my rifle and ran forward. I seized the flag and moved to the front of the 54th's attacking ranks. Despite enemy fire, I made it to the top of the fort. Within a minute, I planted the colors on the fort's inner ground. There, bullets and grapeshot flew all around me. But soon I found myself alone with only the dead and wounded."

Carney started coughing but recovered and continued. "To my left, I noticed a group of soldiers advancing toward me. At first, I thought they might be Union troops but with flashes of gunfire, I realized too late that the oncoming troops were Confederate forces. I said to myself, 'The Rebs are never going to get their hands on the regiment's flag.'

"I wound up the colors and made my way down the 30-foot

wall. I have slid and half ran down the embankment. I ended up in a trench that was waist-deep in water. I was pinned down but I made a break for it. When I did, a bullet hit me in the right leg. I soon was hit by a second bullet in the right arm—moving in retreat, another shot struck me. I saw a Union soldier coming in my direction. I hailed him asking, 'What's your regiment?'

"He said, 'I'm with the 100th Regiment of New York. Sir, can I help you carry the flag?'

"'No, I told him. 'I can't give the colors to anyone except a member of the 54th.'

"Together we struggled back. Another bullet grazed my head. Half crawling on one knee, I stumbled to our lines. Before I collapsed, I said, 'Boys, I only did my duty; the old flag never touched the ground.' "

Carney said, "Mizz Harriet, you and I know as everyone else does, that the battle for Fort Wagner's was the nation's test to see if the black man would fight in the face of the enemy. We did, Harriet. We all did. We pushed open the gates of hell. We faced the devil himself. We broke the chains of slavery. I don't know what else to say, except that I do believe I saw so many dead soldiers that the angels carrying them to heaven must have had broken wings."

Harriet reached over and touched Carney's forehead. She said, "From a distance, I saw the rain of blood and heard the screams of soldiers. And then we saw the lightning, and that was the guns; and then we heard the thunder, and that was the big guns; and then we heard the rain falling, and that was blood falling; and then we came to get in the crops, it was the dead men that we reaped."

Harriet continued, "It's been reported that over half the 54th regiment are dead or wounded including the noble Colonel Shaw. I know the bravery of the 54th will have a ripple effect. I do believe thousands of black men will now join the Union army. Lincoln will know what's been done here."

Harriet then reached into her straw basket and pulled out a

bouquet of wildflowers. "These," she said, "are for you. Wildflowers grow and don't need instructions or a plan for their lives. They don't ask why, or where, or how. They are planted right where they need to be. You were placed here by the heavens for a reason. Your desire to carry the flag, when death was all around you, was planted in your heart. So rest easy, William Carney, and know you have done your sacred duty."

We could see that Carney's eyelids were starting to lower with exhaustion. I walked softly away. Harriet stood watch over the sleeping William Carney softly humming *The Battle Hymn of the Republic.*

Chapter 8:
A Whisper Of
Something Else

THE GOOD BOOK SAYS THE Lord giveth and the Lord taketh away. The number of dead and wounded was beyond belief. Many were quickly assigned to burying the departed. There was great care throughout the Union ranks in handling soldier's remains and personal property that would be sent home to wives and family.

After the battle, Union personnel worked hard to maintain order and right itself after such staggering losses. As nurses, we cared for the wounded and gave hope; sometimes miracles happened, but not for me. Will was admitted to the military's main hospital. I was relieved of my nursing duties as my friends and hospital administrators heard of my husband's condition.

I ran up the steps of the hospital and the sight of wounded and smell of death was overwhelming. As I entered the ward, I saw that two surgeons were examining Will. He searched their faces looking for answers. With an anxious look he asked, "Do you think, I'll pull through, sir?"

Looking down, one surgeon answered, "I hope so, Sergeant." There was a moment of silence and a shadow crossed the surgeon's face. There hung in the air a whisper of something else.

After greeting Will, I quickly decided to follow the surgeons on their rounds and asked, "Which men in the room probably were suffering the most?"

I was shocked to see that they both glanced at Will. The older surgeon said, "Every breath he breaths is like the stab from a knife because a ball pierced his right lung. It broke ribs. There is no telling the amount of damage that's been done. He has to lie on his back or he will suffocate. It will be a hard and long struggle to the end."

"To the end? Do you mean he is going to die? He's a young and strong. Can't you operate and save him?"

"I wish I could, nurse, but there isn't much hope. There are so many wounded soldiers who urgently need surgery that I'm asking you to tell him that news. If you can, find out who his family is and notify them immediately. He won't last more than a day or two."

"Only a day … or two … ?" The two surgeons moved on down the ward. I felt my body collapsing from the inside out. The room was suddenly spinning. I grabbed onto a chair nearby and sat down. I could have sat on the spot for days and cried but not then, not with Will at the end of the ward. He might see me and I didn't have the heart to face the truth or tell him anything yet.

I murmured, "It wasn't fair. It wasn't fair. The army needed men like Will, men who are strong and brave who fight for liberty and justice. I can't give him up. I'm his bride." I started praying and bargaining with God, hoping that something would change the horrible news and make my grim task unnecessary.

When I had the courage to return to his bedside, Will looked lonely and forsaken. I saw tears rolling down his face. I took him in my arms and said, "Let me help you."

"Thank you, Cece. I don't want to be any trouble. There are so many other soldiers here that need your help."

"Will, I'm your wife and I love you dearly." I felt him softly touch my dress, as if an assurance that I was there.

I assisted on Will's ward whenever I could, but I was devoted to all his needs. I helped with the bathing and bandaging his wounds. He would lean against me as I dressed the wound. Tears rolled down his face from pain, but no one saw them fall but me. He could not talk much because his breath was precious. He now only spoke in short sentences and in a whisper.

Will and I had talked about his family before, but there now seemed to be a sense of urgency for him to share details that I might use to identify each member's face and personality. He began, "My mother is the rock of our family. Her name is Charlotte and she is tall like me. She learned from her minister how to read and write and she taught all my family.

"My brother Ed is two years younger than me and people say he's my twin. My two sisters are now schoolteachers at out church. Jenny's the oldest. She loves to garden and Sara my younger sister is becoming a good cook. I want you to meet my family and I know they will love you. Our farm is not far from Buffalo, New York. We'll go there when all of this is over."

I could see from his feverish face that he was becoming weary as he gasped for air. "Of course we will, my dear," I said, "as soon as this is over. I think we should write to them. Do you think you're up to saying something now? If not, I can fill in with news of the war."

"Cece, you go ahead and write to them, but I want you to tell them that we were married. Tell them about you and your brother Lou, Tilly, Harriet and the bravery of the 54th. My mother will want to know the name of the minister who married us, so be sure to write out Reverend Charles Smith's name. She will want to write to him and thank him, you know."

I could see that Will's eyes were lowering in exhaustion. His breath was much more labored. I worked with cold cloths and sponges to keep his fever down. I waited till there was a period of merciful sleep to take pen to paper and begin the letter to his family. It would not just be a friendly letter about our recent marriage, but the shattering words of his looming death. I needed to tell his mother what an honorable man he was and the affection that I had for him. The hospital was now the headquarters for all mail and I quickly delivered the letter to the office on the first floor.

After returning to Will's bed, I saw him grimacing in pain and asked the surgeon for more pain medication. It was limited, but it was at least something. I said, "While you were resting, I wrote the letter we talked about to your family and sent it. I did tell them we were married and that you were injured in the battle."

Will turned to me and said, "I'm a little sorry," he said, "that I was not wounded in the front. It looks cowardly to be hit in the back." He asked me, "Do you think this will be my last battle?"

It was the hardest question that I have ever been asked as he looked earnestly at me for the truth. I softly said, "Yes, Will. I do."

He seemed a little startled at first then a shudder went through his being. He turned away as a tear rolled down his cheek. He then said, "I hope an answer comes soon from the letter you wrote to my family. Cece, we have not spent a matrimonial life together. I so dearly wanted to be your loving husband." He slowly lowered his head and turned his face to the side.

Night came softly and I slept in a chair by his bedside. In the early morning I could see the gray veil of death lowering over his face. I gently wiped away the increasing streams of sweat and placed cold cloths on his forehead and wet his fever-cracked lips. I fanned away the flies and waited. I could do little else but hope and pray. Each breath was fought for with huge spasms. His hands were clenched for the fight, but his limbs grew cold.

Many men around the room began to wake and gather around his bed as his massive gasps for air echoed in the room. He suffered for hours. All were watchful and filled with pity for such a young man. He squeezed my hand and held it tight. I will never forget as he whispered to me with a face that begged to be remembered, "I love you Cece."

He lapsed into merciful unconsciousness and slowly gave up his last battle, and died. He still held on to my hand very tight, so tight that I could not pull it away. Another soldier said, "It's not good, ma'am, for dead and living flesh to be held together too long. Let me help you."

With that the soldier gently released my hand away as I in my grieving numbness, could not. My hand was cold and stiff with deep finger marks across the back—-no more to feel Will's warm love.

When the news of his death passed throughout the hospital, many came to pay their respects for such a gallant sergeant of the famous 54th. Many soldiers quietly saluted with pride such a strong warrior. Will lay in state for a half an hour which is very unusual for that busy place when so many patient beds were needed. Several of his friends from the 54th came to take him and acted as a color guard for his body.

I followed behind them and waited for my dear husband to be placed in a pine coffin. It was the end of the love of my life. I kept repeating his name. "Will, William, Will—I love you."

I know he heard me.

Will was buried . . . and days later, I picked violets and placed them on my beloved's grave. Will told me on our wedding day that the violets in my bridal bouquet would always remind us of our dreams and of our future. I now felt I had no future and would forever live in the past.

It wasn't long after Will's death that I saw Tilly. There she was eight days after the battle, waiting in same line that I was in at the hospital for mail. We hugged and Tilly said, "I've been helping in General Hospital Number 10. Lots of the survivors of the 54th were sent there. My supervising nurse is Esther Hawks. She is a real surgeon, but because she's a woman the army won't let her practice like one. Her husband, John Hawks, is a surgeon, so they work together. I help out on their wards." Tilly then lowered her head and with a grimace on her face said, "I'm afraid to ask, but how are Will and Lou?"

"My brother was wounded pretty badly during the battle, but he is recovering. I'm trying to recover too."

"What you mean, Cece? Were you shot?"

"No, I mean—and this is so hard to say—Will died a week ago. I know he suffered terribly and the surgeons couldn't do anything to help him."

"Oh, Cece, I am so sorry. William was such a wonderful man. In the past, I've heard the men in Company D sharing stories about his bravery. Some men are just bound to lead and it seems they put themselves at the front of the battle line and suffer for it. Both of you were so suited to each other. Anyone looking at you as a couple could see that you were glowing with light and love. Is there something I can do to help you?"

"Not really, not right now. I just try to keep my head up and help any way I can. That is what Will would have wanted. Seeing you helps me too. Knowing you care. I have been waiting in line here hoping to get a letter back from his family. Even though Will's gone, I do want so much to be a part of his family. I hope they will let me do that."

"I'm waiting here for a letter too from my special soldier's family. I haven't said anything to you, but I found me a real kindly man from the 54th. He is in a different company than your brother or Will. We met a few weeks ago. He told me about his family in Virginia and he can read and write.

"He wrote his family about me and told them that he was going to marry me. I never said much to you and Harriet about him 'cause it all happened so fast, but he was my fiancé. With all the short time between battles we jumped the broom the old-fashioned way of hitching up. We wanted to have a preacher marry us like you did, but there just wasn't time. We said vows to each other and hoped the Lord wouldn't mind. His name is John Wilkens—Private John Wilkens."

"Oh, that's wonderful news, Tilly. I am so happy for you. But I have to ask, did he survive the battle?"

"I don't know, Cece. I can barely say the words … I've been told that John is missing in action or captured. No one has found him yet. I am just beside myself with fear. I've asked everyone I know, but no one seems to know much of anything. All they say is that the military is doing everything they can to locate him. I don't know what to do next or who to talk to."

"Oh, Tilly, I am so sorry. Maybe we should try and talk to Harriet about him. What company was he in?"

"He was in Company B. Thank you, Cece. I come here every day and look for information and maybe for letters from his family in Virginia. If you can, please talk to Harriet about him."

I visited Harriet soon after seeing Tilly. She looked more exhausted than I had ever seen her before. She said, "Cece, I am so sorry to hear about Will and sorry that I could not see him before he passed. There was so much chaos and I have been under strict orders since the battle. Visiting you was impossible for me. I know Will was one of the bravest soldiers that I've ever met. I was told that he remained behind fighting during the battle so that the wounded under his command could make their retreat."

"Oh, Harriet, thank you for saying that. Will never told me what happened on the battlefield. My life will never be the same without him. I know, Harriet, for all of us, the world has changed. You look so worn out. How are you?"

"I've been spying for the Union, day and night. We lost a lot of men and the military is trying to find them and many have been captured. I've been working with my scouts to find out where the Union prisoners are being held."

"That's one of the reasons that I am here. I saw Tilly yesterday and she told me she met a soldier in the 54th named John Wilkens from Company B of the 54th. Tilly said he was her fiancé and they jumped the broom. So far he is not listed among the dead and she doesn't know if he is missing or was taken prisoner. Tilly wanted me to ask you if you knew anything about the prisoners."

"All I know so far is this," Harriet said, "under the flag of truce on the day after the assault, there was a chain of Union sentinels dividing the Rebs from us. These men saw a lot and have been able to say who the men were that were taken prisoners. Those that were captured were sent to Charleston to the Washington Racecourse. It's a temporary prison in the heart of the city. I'll get back to you as soon as I can about him. You take care, Cece, and your brother too. I am so very sorry about Sergeant Will."

We hugged and I quickly left to get back to the hospital tents. So many beds needed to be changed and meals had to be delivered. I anxiously waited to hear what Harriet might find out. Earlier, my brother had told me scary things about prisoners-of-war and pretty much what happened to them. Within a day, Harriet returned with the news. She said, "I've learned that Private John Wilkens was taken prisoner and is at that horse park in Charleston. One of the sentinels on the line the day of the truce knew him and spotted him."

I told Tilly the terrible news. After that day, I didn't see her in the hospital for a long time. I asked other nurses about her but they said she was reassigned to a military commissary on St. Helena Island. I thought that was odd because I knew how much she loved helping the 54th soldiers. But in war times, everything changes on a moment's notice. Tilly and I belonged to the army and our lives were not our own.

Chapter 9:
Roses At The Racecourse

A FTER THE BATTLE FOR FORT Wagner, my brother slowly recovered from his wounds. He had been shot in the arm and chest. With all the newly arrived wounded, I spent as much time as I could helping him to mend, but on off duty days I would visit Will's grave.

Harriet spied, cooked, and nursed soldiers for another year. But in May of 1864 she applied for leave from her duties at Port Royal. Years of nonstop wartime service caught up with her. She was exhausted and weak, and suffered powerful bouts of sleeping sickness. "I gotta go home, Cece. If I can, I'll come back."

Harriet never did. She received an army pass to go home for a time. Soon she returned to her duties thinking she would be back in the South. But the army persuaded her that she was needed more to care for the wounded at Fortress Monroe in Virginia. I continued my nursing and cooking for the Union Army of the South.

The news about Colonel Shaw was terribly painful. We heard that Confederate General Hagood said, "I will bury him in a common trench, with the blacks that fell with him." It was reported that Shaw's body was stripped to his under clothing, paraded through the Rebel fort, and thrown into a trench with twenty-five of his fellow soldiers that were buried on top of him. By military protocol, an officer's body was always returned to his commanders. But as everyone knew, it was a way for the Confederates to show disdain for Colonel Shaw.

Colonel Shaw's father wrote to his son's commanders and his words were posted on notice boards, "We can imagine no holier place than that in which he lies among his brave and devoted followers, nor wish him better company—what a bodyguard he has!"

We knew with General Lee's surrender at the Appomattox Courthouse on April 9, 1865, that the bloody Civil War was over. With the news we were shouting "Hallelujah." Drums and gunfire echoed in the camps. The city of Charleston surrendered on April 10, 1865. But five days later the wretched news came that Lincoln was assassinated. There was a hush in the army barracks with the soft, muffled sounds of sobbing. We were a fatherless nation.

Rumors began to spread about a parade. Everyone was talking about a full brigade of 3,000 Union soldiers, including the 54th Massachusetts, were going to be in a military parade in Charleston at the Washington Racecourse on May 1, 1865. Was it about Lincoln? Was it about the end of the war?

Lou came by to see me on Sunday and began, "Cece, we found out what the parade is about. We've known that the Confederates converted the Washington Racecourse in Charleston into a prison. The Rebs imprisoned hundreds of Union soldiers there. The prisoners slept outside with no coverings in the open, with no protection from all the crawling things down here. Most starved to death in that God-awful place. But the most dreadful thing is that the Rebs buried 257 Union men in a mass grave over by the judges' stand."

"They told us that missionaries and abolitionists from the North came to Charleston a couple weeks ago. They went to the black churches and asked for volunteers to dig up those soldiers and rebury them. You know Americans never like soldiers to be treated so badly. Now there's going to be a special service and parade to honor those prisoners on Monday. They told us to get our uniforms cleaned and our boots polished."

Lou went on and said, "Today being Sunday, some of those missionaries wanted to see the 54th Regiment. It sounds like we've earned a big reputation up north since the Battle of Fort Wagner. One of the men who dug up those soldiers is named Sam. He's been talking today about what happened over at headquarters. Do you want to go meet him?"

"Yes, I do. I'm sure I can go," I said, "but I got to check with the other nurses."

"One more thing, Cece. I've heard some news about your friend Tilly. I've heard that ever since the surrender of Charleston, she's been transferred back here from St. Helena. She's been seen at the horse park every day looking over the fences where the prisoners of war were buried behind the judges' stand. Friends tell me she's been watching them dig up those soldiers. It's an awful site and the smell is terrific."

"Oh, no! I heard rumors that the prisoners from the Battle of Fort Wagner were buried there, including her special soldier from the 54th. Was Tilly alone?"

"I heard sometimes she has a little boy with her. She stands there for hours while the digging goes on and talks to no one."

"Oh, Lordy. I hope she's all right. I will have to try and find her."

"I think that might be a good idea, 'cause folks say she looks like a farmer's scarecrow—all bones."

In a little while Lou and I were at regimental headquarters and saw a dozen men talking to regiment officials. Lou spotted a husky young man and led me over to where he was standing. Lou shook hands with him and said, "Hello, Sam. I was listening to you earlier when you were talking about what happened to the prisoners. This is my sister, Cece. She is a cook and nurse with the army. Can you tell her what happened at the Washington Racecourse?"

"Sure," said Sam. "I am a member of the Patriotic Association of Colored Men. A couple weeks ago, an abolitionist from the

North, named James Redpath, and a dozen missionaries came to Charleston. They asked for volunteers from the city's black churches to help rebury 257 Union prisoners buried by the Confederates in a mass grave. They wanted to give those soldiers a proper Christian burial. Twenty-eight of us volunteered. At the time, I went home and talked to my family about what I was going to do.

"My mama, when she heard me telling her about it, was real mad. She didn't want me getting mixed up in anything that might cause trouble. She already heard the neighbor ladies talking about the prison at the racecourse and about how those men suffered in that pig pen. Ever since the battle of Fort Wagner, we heard rumors that those soldiers looked like scarecrows and were left outside day and night on that track. There were stories how they had hardly anything to eat and were terribly abused—worse than most slaves.

"My mama didn't understand why I wanted to do this. I told her those soldiers were thrown in a shallow grave over by the grandstand—all together with no coffins. I told her that I believed that my helping out with reburying those men, was a fine way for us to show our respect for what those poor Union soldiers sacrificed for us.

"Then my mother reminded me that we never bury our dead in pine coffins. We bury our dead late, by the light of pine torches. No master ever allowed us to stop working to bury anybody.

"I told her that I knew that, but it was a way of showing that what was done to them soldiers wasn't right, and it was a way of showing that what was done to all of us—for all them years, wasn't right either. That horse park represented all the enslavers with their terrible power over all of us. There's twenty-eight of us members of the Patriotic Association of Colored Men and the Friends of the Martyrs, that were planning to rebury them soldiers. I said, 'I know things like this ain't easy, mama. Everyone is gonna bring flowers for the graves. I want you to do that too.'

"She said, 'How is that going to help? I never heard of putting flowers on graves of people you never knew.'

"I said, 'James Redpath and the northern missionaries with us men, decided to do it. We want to start a tradition about honoring those soldiers by decorating their graves with flowers.'

"My mama came around to my thinking, but I want to tell you, Lou and Cece, I worked day and night digging. It was a God-awful job but I think it was mighty important to help those poor soldiers get with the Lord. If you are at the parade tomorrow, Cece, come meet my family. My little sister Alice will be there. She grows flowers. I think she'll share some of her roses with you."

"I'd like that, Sam," I said. "I would like to get flowers to put on the soldiers' graves. I'll look for you and my brother tomorrow after the parade. I'll pack a picnic lunch for all of us."

On Monday, lots of us nurses and cooks went to see the parade. I heard there were 10,000 people at the Washington Racecourse and by chance I saw my old friend Tilly in line to get into the horse park. She looked frightfully thin and was holding a little boy in her arms. I think he might have been close to two years old.

The crush of people was overwhelming, but I managed to nudge my way over to her. I grabbed her hand and could tell her whole body was shaking. I asked, "Tilly, I've missed you so much. How are you and who's this little boy?"

"Cece, I am sorry about not getting in touch with you. I just couldn't. This little boy is mine, and his name is John Wilkens Jr. You know what that means. He is mine from my beau Private John Wilkens who died at this horse park."

"I'm so sorry about John and what happened to him, but that's why we are all here today—to honor him. Oh gosh Tilly, you had a baby—a little boy. You are so blessed. I think he looks like you. He's got your smile and your dimples. How wonderful. I bet he's a sweet angel, but who's been helping you care for your son? Are you still working for the army?"

"Well, yes and no. For a while I was on St. Helena. Then the army sent me to some of the other Sea Islands along the coast of South Carolina to help out. I met there a real nice lady by the name of Charlotte Forten, who's a teacher and nurse for the army. She's been teaching me lots of things. Don't you worry about me, Cece. I've had some contrabands helping me out with my little John, and I've been cooking and doing mending at night. I heard about the prisoners here being reburied so I've been coming here every day. It breaks my heart to know what happened to these men including my poor John. Is Harriet here?"

"No, Harriet went back home to rest for a while because she was so worn out tending to all the suffering here. You look mighty tired too. Can I take you back to where you are living and we can talk about all of this in a more quiet spot?"

"No, Cece, I'm here today maybe for the last time. Me and my son are going to a new home. I've asked for a transfer and we're going to Virginia. We are going to John's folks. They agreed to help me out and want to see their grandson. The army sent out letters to the families of soldiers missing in action and prisoners-of-war. John's father will be here today. He came by train.

"I am meeting him for the first time over by the grandstands. I'm wearing this fancy hat so he can recognize me. I hope his family will like me. Cece, I need a family. I never had much of a family. My son looks so much like his father, I am sure they will welcome him, but I hope they will welcome me too. I'm going by train back with John's father to Charlottesville, Virginia. I'm also here to say a few good-byes. If I can, I want to honor John in some way by laying flowers on an unknown soldier's grave. I know he would like that. Is your brother better?"

"Lou is here, and he will be in the parade. Oh, Tilly, I'm sorry for all of this. It just makes me cry to think about you and what you been through and knowing how much I will miss you. Soon the 54th will be disbanded and we will be mustered out of the army. I will miss you terribly. You're one of my true friends. Do you want to walk with me and find a place to watch the parade?"

"No. I can't, Cece. I got to go and find John's father right now. I'll be leaving with him soon." For a moment, Tilly and I hugged and we said with our teary eyes—good-bye.

"I love you, Tilly."

"I love you, Cece. I'll send you a letter."

"I don't want to lose you, please keep in touch with me somehow and let me know where you're at."

With that, Tilly pushed through the crowds away from me and was gone from my sight. I felt like I lost my friend forever, and not just in the crowd.

The parade started promptly at 9:00 a.m. There were hundreds of white and black citizens marching behind what looked like all the children in the city. They were carrying baskets of flowers, wreaths, and small crosses. I couldn't count how many I saw. It made me dizzy. Around and around the racecourse they went singing patriotic songs.

Then in streamed the Union army in strict cadence with a precision of military veterans. They performed a double column march around the track three times with drums and buglers sounding off. They were a sight to see in their blue uniforms and brass buckles. There were military salutes to senior officers and to the fallen soldiers. I saw the 34th, the 104th from the garrison at Beaufort, and the famous 54th Massachusetts Volunteers, including my brother.

Sam was walking with the Patriotic Association of Colored Men and important looking officials. In the grandstands were politicians, black missionaries, and Union officers giving speeches. I listened for a while then met up with Sam and Lou. I pulled Lou aside and told him I saw Tilly and what she said. We both agreed to keep a look-out for her.

Sam said, "I can't find my mother just yet, but this is my sister, Alice. Alice, I want you to meet Lou who is in the famous 54th Massachusetts and his sister Cece who is a nurse and cook with the Union army. Alice, do you have flowers that Cece could have today? I told her you might help her out and share some of your beautiful roses with her. But right now I need to go find ma and pa. I think they may be over by the grandstands. Lou do you want to go with me and Cece, could you keep an eye on Alice for a moment?"

"Sure," I said. "Nice to meet you, Alice. Your brother said you grow lots of flowers. I made cornbread and a berry pie. I would like to trade some of these things in my picnic basket for some of your flowers."

"Miss Cece, I would, but my mama has them all. This morning she got me up real early and said, 'Come on, Alice, we're gonna go to a parade in downtown Charleston today. Your brother, and your daddy's 104th Regiment from Beaufort are going to be in it and so is the famous 54th Massachusetts Volunteers.

"I was so excited I put my hair in braids and put on my best dress and Sunday shoes. Mama packed a picnic basket and told me to get her scissors out of her sewing basket, so I asked, 'Why do we need to take scissors to a parade?'

"Then my mama said, 'Alice, honey, we need to take the flowers from your garden. They are for the Union soldiers.'

"That's when my mama cut the flowers from my garden till it looked like the cotton fields that boll weevils ate dry. I kept saying, 'Mama, no! *Please* don't take my flowers—especially not my roses. I look at those flowers every day and think about my granddaddy.'

"You see, Cece, I planted six rose bushes out back next to my mama's vegetable garden with my granddaddy. He showed me how to care for them and he said, 'Alice, roses are the Almighty's way of making our life a little more beautiful.' I grew other flowers like, black-eyed Susans, magnolias, and morning glories, but it was those roses that made my garden special because they came from my granddaddy.

"So then my mama says, 'All right, Alice, we won't cut your roses, but the rest of the flowers are for the soldiers and you'll see why.'

"I cried half-way to the horse park."

Alice then motioned toward a large gathering of people near a tall white fence. She said, "There's my mama and my daddy. Let's go see them. Maybe my mama will give you some of my flowers."

I said, "Yes, I would like that."

Alice and I walked across the horse park and found Alice's parents. Quickly Sam and Lou found them too. "Hello," I said. "My name is Cece and this is my brother, Lou. We just met your daughter and son and wondered if I could trade my cornbread for some of your flowers. Alice said she didn't have flowers, but you might."

"My name is Mary and this is my husband Robert who is in the 103rd U.S. Colored Troops from Beaufort. I do have flowers, but I first wanted to show Alice what we're doing with the flowers cut from her garden."

Mary took Alice's hand and led her to the entrance of the gravesite. It was surrounded by a ten-foot whitewashed fence. We could see that there were so many flowers on the tops, sides, and in between each grave that there was not a speck of dirt anywhere. Over the arched entrance was a sign. Sam said, "The sign reads, 'Martyrs of the Race Course.' One of the missionaries painted it."

"So what are martyrs?" Alice asked.

Sam said, "Martyrs are people who died for someone or a cause they believe in. The men in this cemetery died so you could be free. They were Union soldiers that were captured and died a terrible death in this horse-park prison. Me and twenty-eight other men from the black churches here in Charleston helped give these soldiers a proper Christian burial. We're starting a tradition by decorating the soldier's graves with flowers to honor them. We are calling this, the nation's first Decoration Day."

Alice started to shake. "You never told me that. Nobody ever told me that."

"We thought you knew, with all of us talking about it," said Sam. "It's all right, Alice. We're sorry we didn't explain everything. It all happened so fast. Come on now and help us put the flowers on the graves."

Everyone entered the cemetery gate and began laying flowers on the burial mounds. Alice grabbed her mother's hand and said, "Ma, I forgot something over by the gazebo. Do you think I could take a minute and go get it?"

"All right, Alice, but come right back. We will wait for you," her mother said.

Alice turned to me and in a voice filled with anguish whispered, "Please, Cece, come with me. I've gotta to go back home. It's not far. I need your help. There is something else I need to do right away and it won't take long. Will you come with me?"

In the same moment at the far end of the cemetery, I could see Tilly and her little boy kneeling over a gravesite crushing the flowers around them. I didn't have time to go to her. I wanted to speak to her again, but Alice had already grabbed my hand and was pulling me toward the horse park entrance.

"All right," I said. "I'm coming."

Alice and I slipped away quietly and ran down the deserted streets of Charleston to her home. We went straightaway into her garden.

Alice said, "Cece, see my lovely garden? Some of my roses here are in full bloom and others are just buddin'. I think they must be like the men buried at the horse-park cemetery. I remember what mama did when my daddy went off to fight in the Union army. She pressed rose petals into a handkerchief for him to carry as a reminder about coming home. The soldiers buried in that holy ground need my roses. They are *never* going home."

"So let's get your scissors, cut those roses, and get back quick," I said.

Alice and I cut all her roses and ran back through the streets to the horse park. We found Alice's family. She showed them her beautiful bouquet of red and yellow roses. Her mother looked surprised. "Alice, honey," she said, "I thought you didn't want any of your roses cut, so we didn't do that."

Alice could barely speak from the tears caught in her throat. Trembling she said, "Mama, I'm sorry, so very sorry, about not being kind to the soldiers—and not willing to give something back. I have only *22* roses to give today. But I promise,—I promise Mama—every year, I will grow my roses until I can say that I gave every soldier in this cemetery a beautiful rose."

"Alice," her mother said, "I think those roses gave you a special gift that you never expected, a beautiful lesson in kindness." Alice then hugged her family and Lou and me too. I looked around the racetrack grounds for Tilly, but I did not see her anywhere. I quietly prayed that I would see her again one day.

On the first day of May, 1865, together we laid flowers and twenty-two roses on the holy mounds. We could smell the sweet perfume of hundreds of spring flowers. We heard the hushed sobs of nearby soldier's families. We listened to the children in the nearby grove singing "The Star-Spangled Banner." It was day of gaiety and sorrow, but more than anything else, it was a remembrance by black and white citizens coming together to honor those who died for freedom and for saving the Union of all of these United States.

Chapter 10:
Cookies With Harriet

THE WAR OF THE REBELLION ended. The 54th Massachusetts Volunteers Regiment was disbanded. It took many years for the wounds of war to heal. The land was scarred with open pits from exploding cannon fire. Many cities were in ruins. Blown-out, decaying buildings were reminders of their once former glory. Life shuffled forward with daily concerns for food, shelter, and clean water.

However, it was a new normal that felt good. We were now free and didn't have to fear the master's whip or being sold south. In small ways people started building their new lives. Lou and I returned to Auburn and began piecing our lives back together. Harriet was there too with her mother, father, brothers, and nieces and nephews. I received a short letter from Tilly saying she and her little boy were settled. Over time, Lou and I found marriage partners and each of us had our own children.

There was a sweetness that came with freedom. One was our habit of visiting Harriet. She lived on the outskirts of Auburn. Often "Auntie Harriet" as she was lovingly called in the neighborhood, would invite Lou and me along with our children and more of the neighborhood kids for cookies in her cozy kitchen. We would listen to her stories about her travels on the Underground Railroad sprinkled with some of her adventures as a Union spy. The boys and girls were always curious to hear more. It never failed that one of them would ask about the scar on her forehead.

"Oh, yes," she would say. "Doesn't it look like a flying bird? I got that scar when I was hit in the head with a two-pound weight. An overseer threw it at a runaway slave. He missed him and instead hit me square in the forehead."

"Does it hurt, Auntie Harriet?" a young boy asked.

"Well, yes it does. I've had headaches for a long time. But a few years ago when I was in Boston. I saw a great big building. I asked a man what it was, and he said it was a hospital. So I went right in, and I saw a young man there, and I said, 'Sir, are you a doctor?' and he said he was. Then I said, 'Sir, do you think you could cut my head open?' Then I told him the whole story, and how the head was giving me a powerful sight of trouble lately with achin' and buzzin' so I couldn't get no sleep at night.

"And he said, 'Lay right down here on this here table,' and I did. He didn't give me anything for pain. I refused anesthetic during the operation. Instead I bit on a bullet like the Civil War soldiers did during medical amputations. I just lay motionless as a log, mumbling prayers through my clenched teeth on that bullet. He opened my skull, and raised it up, and now it feels more comfortable. I got up and put on my bonnet and started to walk home, but my legs kind of gave out under me, and they sent for an ambulance and sent me home."

"Mizz Harriet," an older boy said, "you are so brave. Did anyone else hurt you?"

"Yes, when I was a young child my master sent me to work at a nearby home in Dorchester County. I was supposed to learn weaving. But as much as I tried, I never did it right. So they decided to have me check their muskrat traps in the freezing cold river instead. I couldn't let those poor animals be caught, so I would let them go free. I was beaten for that. Eventually from that chilly river water, I got pneumonia. I was sent back home to my mother, Old Rit, who nursed me back from that terrible sickness.

"The first time I was hired out my master, Mr. Brodess, hired me out to Miss Susan. Miss Susan was just plain mean. I was expected to be a maid doing all the work by day and a nursemaid to the baby at night. I was not more than seven years old myself. In order to hold that baby, because of how heavy it was, I had to sit on the floor and rock it over and over and never let it cry. If the child screamed in the night and woke up Miss Susan, I got the rawhide whip.

"On one occasion, Miss Susan told me to dust the parlor. I knew nothing about dusting, but I took the dusting cloth and wiped all the chairs, table, and mantle. Then I swept the floor. Well the dust from that floor, with nowhere else to go, settled again like a white coating all over the furniture. Miss Susan ordered me to do it over and over again at least five times before breakfast, cause it wasn't done right.

"After each time, she beat me bad with her whip. By the last time, I ran away. I ended up at a pig farm and hid out there for three days. I was so hungry that I fought the pigs for their slops. Eventually, I was so starved that I went back to Miss Susan's. They sent me home saying I was useless. But I have the scars from those whippings forever on my back and neck. The whip is a mighty powerful tool for punishment."

"Auntie Harriet," a girl asked, "how many times did you go south to rescue people?"

"Well, I made thirteen trips through forests and swamps, into the South like Moses did in the land of Egypt, to rescue my people. It was always a dangerous task. My good friend and abolitionist, Thomas Garrett, was always worried about me. But I assured Mr. Garrett, that I had great confidence that God would protect me in all my perilous journeys, because I never went on a mission without His consent. I helped many slaves find freedom. 'I was a conductor on the Underground Railroad for eight years, and I can say what most conductors can't say. I never ran my train off the track and I never lost a passenger.'

"On one of my visits to New York, I stayed at the home of Henry Garnet, who was a well-known abolitionist. Now don't confuse those two names—Thomas Garrett and Henry Garnet. Well one night while I was sleeping, I had a vision. Three years before it ever happened, I saw something that was going to come to pass, before it ever did. In the morning I rose up and came downstairs for breakfast singing, *'My people are free! My people are free!'*

'Oh Harriet, Harriet!' Mr. Garnet said. 'You've come to tease us before the time; do cease this noise! My grandchildren may see the day of emancipation of our people, but you and I will never see it.'

"So I said, 'I tell you, sir, you'll see it, and you'll see it soon. My people are free! My people are free.' Three years later when President Lincoln freed us with the signing of the Emancipation Proclamation, there was a lot of rejoicing and jubilee. They asked me why I wasn't celebrating too. I told them, I had my jubilee three years ago. I rejoiced all I could then. I can't rejoice no more.'

"Later I talked to my friend Sojourner Truth. She had met President Lincoln in person. Lincoln told her, 'he had done nothing himself, he was only a servant of the country.' Now, I'm sorry I didn't see Master Lincoln and thank him.'"

"I want to say too that even though the 13th Amendment was passed abolishing slavery, bigotry and injustices went on. I remember a time when I was given leave from my army position in South Carolina to go north to visit my family. I bought a half-fare train ticket from Philadelphia to New York. When I was onboard, the conductor ordered me to the smoking car. I refused to move. I explained that I was working for the government and was entitled to sit wherever I liked. The conductor tried to physically remove me, but I resisted."

"The conductor yelled, 'Come on out of here. We don't carry your kind for half-fare."

"I then told the conductor he was a copperhead. So he started choking me. I told him that I didn't thank anybody to call me a colored person. I am black or Negro and that I was as proud of being a black woman as he was of being white.

"The conductor then called for two other men to remove me from the passenger car. I held on to part of the train's compartment. The men pulled me backward and seizing my arm, broke it. I was then thrown into the smoking car. That further injured my shoulder and broke several of my ribs. It took months for me to heal. So as you know, not everything is healed with just words on paper. It takes time to change the hearts and minds of many folks.

"Lou, I want you to know, that I loved the 54th Massachusetts Volunteers that you joined and I am proud of you for doing it. It made my heart leap with joy when I saw the first black troops marching into the South. During my days with the army, I saw what happened at Fort Wagner when the 54th lost half of their men. Colonel Shaw and the 54th fought with great courage that night."

"It's good to hear you say that Harriet," said Lou. "I know that you were present and fought alongside many men in battle. But I know after the Civil War ended, you kept fighting for the less fortunate of Auburn. You shared your home with the elderly and sick. You even bought more property and built a separate facility to care for them."

"You're right Lou. I used my small savings to purchase a 25-acre parcel next to my present home. When the auction for the property began, I hid in the corner of the room, fearing they would ask me to leave. They were all white men, but me there. There I was like a blackberry in a pail of milk, but I hid in the corner, and no one knew I was bidding. When the auction was over, the auctioneer called out asking. 'All done. Who is the buyer?'

"Harriet Tubman," I shouted.

"When they asked me how I was could possibly pay for the land, I replied, 'I'm going to go home to tell Lord Jesus all about it.' I did end up using my home as collateral and my church helped me out too. With the additional land, I built that home for the elderly and I planted an apple orchard. Now I got a lot of room for my vegetable garden and pig-pens for my pigs.

"I planted that apple orchard because when I was a little girl, I was whipped badly by the overseer. He saw me take one bite out of an apple in the master's apple orchard. I never forgot it and dreamed of a day when I might have all the apples I could eat. I wanted to be sure everyone here in Auburn could enjoy those tasty apples. So, would you like to go outside and pick some apples today? We might even make some apple pies. Would you like to do that children?"

Of course they all agreed and rushed out on that October day. Before we left Harriet's kitchen, I paused to look for a basket and Harriet turned and asked me, "Cece, what was your best memory of our time together in the South?"

"What I remember most, Harriet, were all the times that we stood together. We stood perfectly still so many nights, when the slave catchers and bloodhounds were near. We stood on battlefields and in hospitals looking at frightening wounds trying to say something comforting to terrified soldiers. We stood alongside hundreds of suffering men holding them down when they were about to have arms and legs amputated. We stood over dying men too, holding their hands while they softly slipped away.

"And we stood and cooked for the Union soldiers and the needy contrabands in the terrible heat of those southern nights. But most of all what I remember, was the silly laughter we all had while we stood late at night making those berry pies and root beer. We found home in the smiles when we saw soldiers eating those desserts and talking about their families. Isn't that right, Harriet?"

"Yes, it is," she answered. We both smiled and put on our

homespun shawls. We then went out to pick the new, shiny red apples from her lovely orchard.

Chapter 11:
Touched By Harriet's
Great Heart

HARRIET DIED ON MONDAY, MARCH 10, 1913 from a severe case of pneumonia. Many people including Lou and I came to be with her at the end, but visitation was limited. A few hours before her death, we could hear her faint voice singing, "Swing Low, Sweet Chariot." Late that evening, the chariot arrived to take her home. At the end of her life, present at her bedside was Martha Ridgeway her nurse, and Harriet's friend, Reverend Charles A. Smith, Smith's wife Frances, Eliza Peterson of the Women's Temperance Union, and two of Harriet's great-nephews, Charles and Clarence Stewart. Even though Harriet was possibly 91 years old, her death was a shock to the community and her friends.

Harriet's life was about service and her spiritual life was never far away. One of the last times Harriet attended church, heaven was on her mind. She told the hushed congregation, "I am nearing the end of the journey. I can hear them bells ringing. I can see the angels singing. I can see the hosts a-marching. I can hear someone say, 'There is one crown left and that is for Old Aunt Harriet, and she shall not lose her crown."

A little over a year after her death, Auburn did not forget its favorite daughter. On June 12, 1914, the city where Harriet had spent much of her life, organized a stirring tribute to honor her service to the nation during the Civil War and to the cause of freedom. Mayor Brister issued a proclamation asking for all flags to be flown throughout the city. Through voluntary donations, Auburn's citizens paid for a bronze tablet to celebrate her extraordinary life.

Most of the city's citizens came with their families to honor Harriet. Parents wanted their children to hear more about Auburn's famous "Auntie Harriet". There were speeches and flag waving including a special tribute from Harriet's old friend, Brooker T. Washington. He said, that among her accomplishments, "She had brought the two races nearer together and made it possible for the white race to place a higher estimate upon the black race."

On that beautiful day of celebration, Clarence Stewart, Martha Ridgeway, Reverend Smith and his wife, Lou, I, and other church members decided to share stories about our dear friend Harriet. The ladies of the parish and friends organized a church picnic. We baked Harriet's favorite cookies, cornbread, and pies and brewed her recipe for root beer to share. We did not have prepared speeches, but decided to speak freely about our special memories of Harriet.

"I am sure you heard," I said, "that Harriet was buried with full military honors at Fort Hill Cemetery. On that day, hundreds came to pay their last respects including Lou and me. There were many eulogies given by church members and local dignitaries. Harriet had many important friends like William Seward, Thomas Garrett, William Lloyd Garrison, Wendell Phillips, Reverend Henry Highland Garnet, William Still, Lucretia Mott, and Frederick Douglass, who might have spoken on her behalf, but they all died before she did."

Martha added, "Harriet used to say, 'There's only one more journey for me to take now, and that's to heaven.' I want to tell you that before Harriet slipped into a coma, she said to those around her, 'I go away to prepare a place for you, that where I am you may also be.' "

Martha chuckled and added, "It seems like Harriet was always planning to lead us home in this life or another."

Martha went on, "Mary Talbert, who is a great suffragette, visited with Harriet about a month ago. She said that when she was about to leave, Harriet reached for her hand and holding it tight said, '*Tell women to stand together.*'

"You know, Harriet always had a cause she was fighting for and I do believe she wanted women to have the vote. Even Elizabeth Miller, a leader of a local suffragist group, asked her once, 'Do you really believe that women should vote?' Harriet paused and said, 'I suffered enough to believe it.' "

Lou said, "Harriet was always like family to Cece and me. We were all born and raised in Dorchester County. Even Harriet's friend, Frederick Douglass, came from Talbot County, just northwest of us in Maryland. I heard Douglass once say about Harriet's time of working on the Underground Railroad, 'Tubman's work was to labor in a private way for activities observed only by the midnight sky and the silent stars.' I saw Harriet always working quietly for others. She never liked a lot of public attention, but she was a celebrity. Harriet was recognized where ever she went. She was especially noticed in Auburn where people would point and whisper, 'There goes Harriet Tubman.' "

Reverend Smith said, "Harriet wore herself out caring for others. What set Harriet apart from thousands of runaway slaves was her determination to act. After making her own way to freedom, she quickly made plans to liberate her family, friends, and other fugitive slaves. Things like that were not supposed to happen, but she had an iron will and a courageous heart.

"She bore the scars of slavery on her neck and back all her life. She never sought power and remained poor. At the end of her life, when money was needed to pay for her care and treatment, newspapers in the community ran articles about her circumstances asking for donations. Enough money was raised for Harriet to be placed in her Home for the Aged with a private room."

Reverend Smith added, "It is a shame, but Harriet wasn't paid what she was owed by the government during the years she served in the Union army. When her second husband, Nelson Davis died, she got a small pension of twenty dollars a month from his military service, but Harriet never received a pension for her time in the cause during the Civil War. Not only that, she only drew for herself but twenty days of rations during her years of service. William Seward, one of our Auburn's community leaders and as a U.S. Senator, fought to get her money from the government. They laughed at him and said it was absurd and unrealistic. But Cece, you saw her service to the army."

"Yes," I said. "Harriet fought alongside men in combat and was a Union spy for over two years. I know that during the war, she liked to keep her letters and army dispatches from Colonel Montgomery in her pockets. She did not know how to read and write, but they were more to her than paper and ink. They were a small diary of her life. Over time they became faded and torn but they were never thrown away."

Martha said, "I want to tell everyone here that Harriet was someone who was honored by all of the greats of her time. Her fame even spread overseas. Queen Victoria of England read her biography and being 'pleased with it,' sent Harriet a silver medal that commemorated Victoria's Diamond Jubilee, a white shawl, and an invitation to come to England. Harriet looked at that letter so many times that it was worn to a shadow. That silver medal was buried with her in her coffin. Harriet regretted that she 'didn't know enough to go to England, and never mind that she could not have afforded it.'

"Harriet was also acquainted with Elizabeth Stanton, Lucretia Mott, and Susan B. Anthony, who assisted her financially and materially. These strong women knew Harriet was as a compelling speaker who fascinated her audiences with her stories and challenged them to act. Over time, Harriet was introduced to many writers by her friends, Thomas Higginson and Franklin Sanborn. She was a guest at the homes of Amos Bronson Alcott—the father of Louisa May Alcott, Mrs. Horace Mann, and Ralph Waldo Emerson. They admired and respected her and she felt at ease with them."

Clarence added, "I know that Harriet wasn't bitter about the way she was persecuted because of her race or the pain some caused her. She blamed it on the way those masters were brought up—with a whip in their hands."

Clarence continued, "She started with so little but always did so much. Some people say she was illiterate, but that doesn't mean she was ignorant. Harriet was an entrepreneur and community leader. During the Civil War, she established her own laundry service. She helped build a community wash-house so the contrabands could earn money by washing the army's laundry. She not only contributed to their independence but to their self-respect as well. Here in Auburn, you all know she owned and operated a pig farm, vegetable garden, and managed a home for the aged. She had a very big heart."

Frances Smith nodded and said, "But I'm not sure everyone here knows how hard she struggled to make ends meet. I'm sure you will remember the terrible winter of 1867-68 around here. It was a bad one. Harriet's family had very little food and fuel. Her situation became desperate. She found it necessary to beg for money from her friends in town. The snow piled up. It was difficult to get to from her farm on the outskirts of the city. Her situation was dire.

"Harriet plunged through the snowdrifts and arrived at the home of a white benefactor, Miss Annie. Annie told me Harriet struggled to speak the words and with eyes filled with tears, Harriet asked for a quarter. Annie gave her the needed quarter and notified other Harriet supporters who quickly supplied her with the necessities for her family. But true to her honesty and integrity, Harriet returned that same precious quarter the next Monday."

A church member spoke up and said, "That story reminds me of a time that the vendors at our local market told about Harriet's visit with her empty basket. It seems her mother at times hounded Harriet about food and money to the point that Harriet hid herself in her closet one day to escape her mother's berating. There she had a little talk with the Lord. They said she emerged with a voice of conviction and shouted, 'Put on the large pot. We're going to have soup today.' She then went off to the downtown market.

"It was near the end of the day, and Harriet walked from stall to stall with no money. There a kind-hearted butcher noticed her empty basket and gave her a soup bone. Other vendors followed suit until her empty basket was full. Harriet said she hadn't gone into the closet and shut the door for nothing. It was another "stone soup" moment about her daily struggles to support a large household of dependents and care of her aging parents."

Lou spoke up, "As I remember after the end of the war, Harriet always helped others. I know you know that Harriet didn't have much, she always shared what she did have with other people. She welcomed many folks who were old, sick, or destitute into her home and cared for them including several orphans. Her "last work" as she called it, was to set up a hospital and home for the aged and destitute blacks.

"For many years, you've seen Auntie Harriet looking like a peddler traveling house to house selling her eggs, butter, vegetables, and a few chickens. So many of us would invite her in for tea and something to eat and she would tell her stories about the war and escaping along the Underground Railroad. Harriet would often say to children, 'Learn all you can. No one can take that away what you have in your head.' "

Martha added, "I know being Harriet's nurse, that she had a great faith, a quick wit, and a sense of humor too. Among all the abolitionists of the 1850s, Harriet was the most respected and despised, but I know Harriet was not afraid of death."

Reverend Smith said, "There is so much to be grateful for including the life of our dear friend Harriet. Thomas Garrett once said of her, 'I never met with any person, any color, who had more confidence in the voice of God, as spoken direct to her soul. Harriet's prayer was a prayer of faith and she expected an answer.' That Harriet never lost a passenger on the Underground Railroad, is no less than miraculous. She marched straight into the enemy's camp and did the most dangerous rescues."

Clarence Stewart added, "We have all been touched by Harriet who rose from slavery and carried an outpouring of others with her into the Promised Land. Her great heart was forged in fiery pain but it also molded her fearless passion. Governor Seward once said, 'I have known Harriet long, and a nobler, higher spirit, or a truer, seldom dwells in human form.' "

"Yes," I said. "I know we all witnessed Harriet's strong will. She once said, 'No one was born a slave. We were enslaved by the enslavers. We did not come here by choice. We did not come here by way of Ellis Island. We were forced to be here.' Harriet was a freedom seeker—seeking freedom from the evils of slave trade and their criminal kidnappers.

"I believe we all know that Harriet had a destiny carved out for her and for the nation by the heavens above. She touched all of us with her great heart and I know we can still hear her strong voice urging us to—*Keep Going*. Harriet loved to sing. I can still hear her strong, beautiful voice in my head singing one of the hymns that she sang when she passed the cabin doors letting her people know she was ready to take them north. It goes like this:

I'm sorry, friends, to leave you,
Farewell! Oh, farewell!
But I'll meet you in the morning,

Farewell! Oh, farewell!

I'll meet you in the morning,
When you reach the Promised Land,
On the other side of Jordan,
For I'm bound for the Promised Land.

I guess it's time for all of us to say farewell one more time to Harriet and to each other. But we should remember the times that have gone by and our friend who loved others so much that she would lay down her life for them. Like her Maker above, when Harriet Tubman made a promise to help, she meant it.

Key Dates In The Life Of Harriet Tubman

1822: Araminta "Minty" Ross born in February or early March in Dorchester County, Bucktown, Maryland. Later known as Harriet Tubman.

1827: At age six Harriet is hired out to work for the Cooks. Miss Susan whips Harriet. She is scarred for life.

1833: At the age of twelve or thirteen, Harriet is struck in the head by an iron, two-pound weight. The injury causes serious side effects for the rest of her life.

1844: Married John Tubman, a free-born black man.

1849: Escapes to freedom along the Underground Railroad.

1850: Harriet leads her first group of Maryland slaves to freedom, helping her niece Kessiah and her niece's two children escape. First of thirteen trips to the South to free slaves.

Congress passes the Fugitive Slave Act as part of the Compromise of 1850.

1851: Harriet rescues one of her brothers, his wife, and nine others.

1852: Harriet Beecher Stowe's *Uncle Tom's Cabin* is published.

Harriet moves to St. Catharines, in Canada, a safe haven from the Fugitive Slave Act.

1854: Rescues three other brothers from Thompson's plantation in Maryland on Christmas Eve.

1855-1860: Harriet rescues about seventy individuals in thirteen trips to the South.

1857: Harriet moves to a home in Auburn, New York.

Harriet rescues her parents and brings them to Auburn, New York.

Supreme Court in a case involving ex-slave Dred Scott, rules that slaves are not citizens and have no rights.

1859: Harriet becomes more politically active, giving lectures as an Underground Railroad conductor.

1860: Abraham is elected President of the United States. Harriet makes her final trip to the South in December to help slaves escape.

South Carolina secedes from the Union, quickly followed by Mississippi, Florida, Alabama, Georgia, Louisiana, and Texas.

1861: Harriet briefly returns to Canada as slave catchers look for her in New York.

The Confederate States are formed. The Civil War begins as Confederate guns fire on Fort Sumter in April.

Union General Benjamin F. Butler declares that slaves fleeing to the Union are "contraband" of war and cannot be returned to their Confederate owners.

1862: Union forces invade South Carolina.

Harriet arrives in South Carolina and begins her work as a cook, nurse, laundress, teacher, and spy for the Union army.

Carol A. Trembath

Harriet recruits ex-slaves as spies. Union officers start calling intelligence reports from African-Americans black dispatches.

January 1, 1863: The Emancipation Proclamation declares all slaves in Confederate controlled areas are "forever free".

Congress authorizes the first black regiment—the 54th Massachusetts Volunteers.

On June 2, 1863 under the direction of Colonel James Montgomery, Harriet leads armed forces up the Combahee River and becomes the first woman to lead a U.S. military operation. They free over 700 slaves.

July 3, 1863: General Lee is defeated at Gettysburg, turning the tide of the war for the Union.

July 18, 1863: The Battle of Fort Wagner is fought with the 54th Massachusetts leading the charge.

Colonel Robert Gould Shaw is killed during the battle.

November 8, 1864: 1864: President Lincoln is reelected.

Harriet is given a pass to return home due to exhaustion.

January 31, 1865: Congress approves the Thirteenth Amendment to the Constitution abolishing slavery.

April 9, 1865: General Lee surrenders at the Appomattox Court House, Virginia, ending the Civil War.

April 15, 1865: President Lincoln is assassinated in Washington D.C. at Ford Theater.

Harriet hired to provide nursing services a Fort Monroe in Virginia. On her way home on a passenger train, Harriet is severely injured by a conductor.

Harriet moves back to Auburn, New York.

U.S. Government refuses to pay Harriet for her time served with the Union Army.

1866: Harriet's first husband, John Tubman, dies.

1869: Harriet marries Civil War veteran, Nelson Davis.

1869: Sarah Bradford publishes her first biography, *Scenes in the Life of Harriet Tubman*.

1870: Harriet supports Susan B. Anthony in founding the women's suffragist movement.

1871: Ben Ross, Harriet's father dies.

1880 Harriet's mother, Rit Ross, dies. Tubman farms and runs small brick making business with her husband.

1886: The second book about Harriet, *Harriet Tubman: The Moses of Her People*, is published.

1888: Harriet's second husband, Nelson Davis, dies.

1890s: Harriet becomes more actively involved in the suffrage movement. She attends both black and white suffrage conventions.

1896: Harriet purchases 25-acre parcel next to her property to establish a home and hospital for the homeless and aged.

1897: Queen Victoria honors Harriet with a silver medal, shawl, and an invitation to visit Great Britain.

1890: Harriet Tubman's home for the aged opens.

1903: Harriet transfers ownership of the 25-acre property to the African Methodist Episcopal Zion Church.

1908: The Harriet Tubman Home is opened by the AME Zion Church.

1913: Harriet dies March 10th in Auburn, New York of pneumonia. She is buried next to her brother at Fort Hill Cemetery in Auburn, New York with full military honors..

The Abolitionists

Frederick Douglass, abolitionist, orator, and friend of Harriet Tubman. A wartime adviser to President Lincoln. He often lectured for the American Anti-Slavery Society. From Wikimedia Commons.

William H. Steward, Governor of New York (1839-43), U.S. Senator (1849-61), and U.S. Secretary of State under President Lincoln (1861-1869). Courtesy of Library of Congress.

Henry Highland Garnet, prominent New York black abolitionist (1815-1882). From Wikimedia Commons.

Thomas Garrett – Underground Railroad Operator. He frequently supplied Harriet Tubman with money, shoes, and lodging to continue her missions conducting runaways from slavery to freedom. Courtesy of Library of Congress.

Suffragettes: Lucretia Mott, Susan B. Anthony, Elizabeth Cady. Courtesy of New York Public Library.

Governer John Albion Andrew of Massachusetts, who was the guiding force in the creation of African-American troops including the 54th Mass. Volunteers. From: Wikimedia Commons.

Harriet Beecher Stowe – Author of *Uncle Tom's Cabin*, published 1852. From Wikimedia Commons.

The original cover *Uncle Tom's Cabin*, one of the most influential novels ever written. From Wikimeda Commons.

The signing of the Emancipation
Proclamation by Francis B. Carpenter.
From: Wikimedia Commons.

Abraham Lincoln, 16th President
of the United States of America.
From: Wikimedia Commons.

Frederick Douglass, abolitionist,
orator, and friend of Harriet Tubman.
A wartime adviser to President
Lincoln. He often lectured for the
American Anti-Slavery Society.
From Wikimedia Commons.

Douglass was a runaway slave
who became an important leader
in the fight to end slavery. He
later published an abolitionist
paper called The North Star.
From: Wikimedia Commons.

About Harriet Tubman

Harriet Tubman's tombstone reads, "Heroine of the Underground Railroad, Nurse and Scout in the Civil War, Born about 1820 in Maryland, Died March 10, 1913 in Auburn, N.Y. Servant of God Well Done."

So much could be added to this epitaph. Harriet Tubman's list of nicknames include Minty, Auntie Harriet, Moses, General Tubman, and Underground Railroad Conductor. She was also an abolitionist, humanitarian, spy, cook, teacher, and suffragist. Her day-to-day life shows clues of someone who hummed when she was lonely, preferred to do her work in private, and loved to cook. She dazzled others with her courage, wit, intelligence, military genius, and integrity of character.

Harriet was born into a strong family of faith. Her mother and father, Rit and Ben Ross, gave her the sense of her roots which stretched outward to "her people". Local ministers of Christian faith—Methodist, Catholic and Baptist—molded her beliefs to the higher purpose of the Golden Rule. Harriet was a devout Christian with a strong intuition. She experienced vivid dreams that she said came to her as premonitions from God.

Harriet suffered in her early years, but rose above her horrific childhood to emerge with a will of steel. On September 17, 1849, Harriet ran away north with her two brothers who became frightened, and persuaded her to return to the plantation. However, on October 3, 1849, after learning she would be sold south, Harriet alone made her way to freedom using the Underground Railroad to reach Philadelphia.

In the following years, slowly and determinedly, Harriet brought one group at a time—relatives and other slaves out of bondage. For self-liberators, it was highly unusual to return to the land of their enslavers, risking capture or even lynching to help others seek freedom. Traveling by night and in extreme secrecy, Tubman served as a conductor on the Underground Railroad and never lost a passenger.

It is asserted that she freed three-hundred slaves, but only seventy can be documented. One of the reasons for this difference is that Harriet's trips were not recorded for fear of discovery. However, after gaining knowledge of the Underground Railroad and setting up much of her own network of trusted friends, Harriet gave detailed instructions to nearly all fugitive groups from Dorchester and Carolina Counties about safe routes to the North. After the Fugitive Slave Act was passed, Harriet took her passengers to Canada and helped them to find jobs.

When the Civil War broke out, Harriet worked for the Union army, first as a cook and nurse and later in 1862 as an armed scout and spy. She was a witness to some of the most horrific fighting in the Department of the South. Harriet led a raid up the Combahee River freeing over 700 slaves. And so, on June 1, 1863, she became the first American woman ever to lead an armed raid into enemy territory.

After the war, Harriet retired to her home in Auburn, New York to help her aging parents and family. However, she continued to work and promote women's rights with other leading suffragettes including Susan B. Anthony, Elizabeth Stanton, and Lucretia Mott. Harriet was woman of tomorrow and an icon of American courage and freedom.

"Some have said of the legendary Underground Railroad and its secret system of fictional trains and nonexistent tracks, was one of history's finest symbols of the struggle against oppression, and that it embodied the nation's leading principle: *the quest for freedom.*"

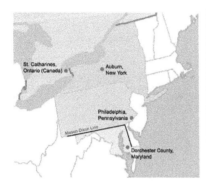 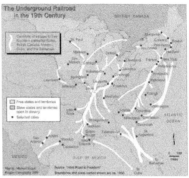

Map of Harriet Tubman's escape route from her home in Dorchester County. From: Wikimedia Commons.

Map of the system of escape routes along the Underground Railroad. Courtesy of New York Public Library.

The International Railway Suspension Bridge near Niagara Falls. First opened in Aug. 1, 1848. Courtesy of Library of Congress.

Harriet Tubman, conductor on Underground Railroad, but also known as Moses. Date unknown. From: Wikimedia Commons.

Harriet posed for this photo in
Auburn, New York.
Courtesy of Library of Congress.

Woodcut of Harriet Tubman holding
a musket, although her weapon of
choice was a pistol.
From: Wikimedia Commons.

Harriet Tubman, abolitionist,
nurse, spy, scout. From:
Wikimedia Commons.

Harriet Tubman, circa 1896-1898.
Courtesy of New York Public Library.

Harriet Tubman Portrait. Harriet escaped slavery and abuse to lead many to freedom on the UGRR. Courtesy of New York Public Library.

Harriet Tubman, circa 1908. Photographer: Ernsberger, Auburn, New York. Photo: late 1860's. Courtesy of New York Public Library.

Harriet Tubman, the photo was taken shortly before her death, circa 1912. Courtesy of Library of Congress.

Margaret Stewart Lucas and daughter Alice Lucas Brickler, circa 1900. Courtesy of New York Public Library.

Harriet Tubman's family. Left to right: Harriet, adopted daughter Gertie Davis, Nelson Davis, Lee Cheny, "Pop" Alexander, Walter Green, Auntie Sarah Parker, and grand-niece Dora Stewart. 1887-1888. Courtesy of New York Public Library

Eliza Brodess' runaway advertisement of Minty (Harriet Tubman) and her brothers, Ben and Harry (Henry), Courtesy of Bucktown Village Foundation & James W. Meredith Family.

Confederate torpedoes (mines) in the Combahee River.
From: Wikimedia Commons.

Contrabands: Newly released slaves at Beaufort, South Carolina, lined up outside a contraband school.
From: Wikimedia Commons.

Harriet Tubman Residence
Auburn, New York.
From: A Traveling She
Goes/Wordpress.

Harriet Tubman Home for
the Aged, Auburn, New York.
From: Wikimedia Commons.

Harriet worshiped regularly at
Thompson African Methodist
Episcopal Zion Church in Auburn,
New York.
From: Auburn publication.

General Store in Bucktown,
Maryland. Site of near-fatal blow to
Harriet's head.
From: Wikimedia Commons.

The First Memorial Day

THE CIVIL WAR BEGAN IN Charleston, South Carolina with the firing on Fort Sumter, on April 12, 1861. At the end of the war on May 1, 1865, the formerly Confederate controlled city of Charleston would be the site of another memorable event involving 10,000 people. However, this time, it would be to honor Union soldiers. This occasion would later quietly reverberate throughout history.

During the final year of the Civil War, the Confederates converted the Washington Racecourse and Jockey Club into an outdoor, prisoner-of-war camp. There, Union soldiers were held in deplorable conditions in the interior of the track. Two-hundred fifty-seven men died of exposure and disease. The Confederate soldiers hastily buried them on the grounds, in a mass grave behind the grandstand.

Among the first troops to enter Charleston and receive its surrender were the 21st U.S. Colored Infantry under the command of Lieutenant Colonel A. G. Bennett. Charleston was a city in utter ruin. By late February, the city was largely abandoned by its white residents due to a prolonged siege, fires, and bombardment.

After the fall of the city, Charleston's former slaves who had remained in the city and had witnessed the suffering at the prison, conducted a series of commemorations. Twenty-eight black workmen went to the Washington Racecourse and reburied the Union soldiers properly. They built a high fence around the new cemetery. Workers whitewashed the fence and built an archway over the entrance on which they inscribed the words, "Martyrs of the Race Course".

The black Charlestonians in cooperation with missionaries and teachers from the North, then staged on the former slaveholders' property an unforgettable parade and celebration involving 10,000 people. The symbolic site of the property and its history, was not lost on the freed people.

A *New York Tribune* correspondent witnessed the event and described it as, "A procession of friends and mourners as South Carolina and the United States never saw before." However, this historic event was overshadowed by the grief and chaos of Lincoln's assassination two weeks earlier on April 15, 1865. Over time the story was forgotten and repressed by the South.

A few years ago, David W. Blight, a Yale professor and an award-winning author of American history, discovered in the Harvard University archives, uncatalogued writings of Union soldiers regarding the first Decoration Day. In the third chapter of his book, *Race and Reunion,* David W. Blight states, "In Charleston, South Carolina, where the war had begun, the first collective ceremony involving a parade and the decoration of the graves of the dead with spring flowers, took place on May 1, 1865. Blight states:

"The war was over and what is now called 'Memorial Day' had been founded by African Americans in a ritual of dedication and remembrance."

Thirteen years later after this stupendous event, Frederick Douglass spoke at a Memorial Day gathering in New York City in 1878. He proclaimed, "The war was not just a struggle of mere sectional character, but a war of ideas, a battle of principles. It was a war between the old and the new, slavery and freedom, barbarism and civilization ... and in dead earnest for something beyond the battlefield."

The "Martyrs of the Race Course" cemetery is no longer in

Charleston. In the late 1880s, the Union dead who were so honored by the black population, were disinterred and reburied at the National Cemetery in Beaufort, South Carolina, with many gravestones marked as "unknown". The original site is now a public park. It was named after Wade Hampton, a former Confederate General, Governor of South Carolina, and known white supremacist.

"By their labor, their words, and their solemn parade on their former owner's racecourse, black Charlestonians created for themselves, and for us, the Independence Day of a Second American Revolution."

–David W. Blight

Grandstands on the north side of the Washington Racecourse, Charleston, S.C. During the closing days of the Civil War, the area was used as a prisoner-of-war camp. Courtesy of Library of Congress

This April 1865 photo shows the graves of Union soldiers who died at the Washington Racecourse prison camp in Charleston, North Carolina which later was renamed Hampton Park. Courtesy of Library of Congress

The ladies club house on the north side of the course, was errected in 1836. The grandstands at the racetrack was designed by Charles F. Reichart. Preservation Society of Charleston

Pictured bandstand on the grounds of the Washington Racecourse. In 1835, part of the Gibbes' plantation was acquired by the South Caroliina Jockey Club, a group that developed the Washington racetrack. Courtesy of Library of Congress

Charleston, South Carolina, in ruins, 1865. Photo by George N. Barnard, Hallmark Cards, Inc.

Charleston, South Carolina, ruins of the railway station, 1865. From: Wikimedia Commons

A marker in Hampton Park in Charleston, S.C., commemorates the 1865 honoring of the Union soldiers who died at a Confederate prisoner of war camp on the site.

Many historans contend that the dedication of the city where the Civil War began, marks the first Memorial Day observance in the United Statees. From: Bruce Smith, Assoc. Press.

Colonel Robert Gould Shaw And the 54ᵀʰ Massachusetts Volunteers

ROBERT GOULD SHAW WAS RECRUITED in March of 1863 at the age of twenty-five, to command the first all-black regiment—the 54th Massachusetts Volunteers. Early in 1863, the prestigious regiment was organized by Massachusetts Governor John Albion Andrew. Andrew requested and received the consent of the War Department to form a regiment of free Northern blacks to serve for three years.

The recruitment effort extended across fifteen northern states and Canada enlisting a total of 1,007 black infantrymen. Thirty-seven white senior officers commanded the 54th. The regiment's sergeants and corporals were black and provided a link between the rest of the enlisted men and their officers. The regiment included the two sons of abolitionist Frederick Douglass, Charles and Lewis, as well as the grandson of Sojourner Truth.

Colonel Shaw grew to respect his men and believed that black soldiers would fight as well as white soldiers. However, many doubted that black men would make good soldiers. Shaw was eager to get his men into action to prove them wrong. When he learned that black soldiers were to receive less pay than whites, Shaw and his men led a boycott of all wages until the inequality was rectified.

The regiment's first skirmish was with Confederate troops at James Island, South Carolina on July 16, 1863. However, their true call to history was their assault on Fort Wagner. Shaw and his men were chosen to lead the attack on Fort Wagner. On July 18, 1863, Colonel Shaw readied 600 men of the 54th for an assault. The soldiers had a sense that they were in the midst of making history with their willingness to die if necessary for this cause.

During the assault Colonel Shaw fought and bravely urged his men onward. Shaw was one of the first to scale the walls and was killed in the charge. Some Confederate reports claim his body was shot seven times, with the fatal wound from a rifle bullet to the chest. The 54th Massachusetts lost 315 men of the regiment's number of 600. The wider battle involved two full brigades of Union soldiers and a total fighting unit of 10,000 men. In all, 1,515 Union soldiers were killed, captured, or wounded.

The 54th proved that they were as brave as anyone, black or white. The first recorded praise of their heroic assault came from the enemy, Lieutenant Aredalle Jones saying, "That morning the Negroes gallantly fought bravely and were led by one of the bravest colonels that ever lived."

Following the battle, a Union party, under the flag of truce, requested the return of Colonel Shaw's remains. However, the Confederate General Johnson Hagood refused to return Shaw's body. To show contempt for the officer who led black troops, Hagood had Shaw's body buried in a mass grave with many of his men. Following the battle, Hagood returned the bodies of the other Union officers who had died, but left Shaw's buried in the mass grave saying, "Had he been in command of white troops, I should have given him an honorable burial; as it is, I shall bury him in the common trench with the blacks that fell with him."

Rather than considering this intended insult by the Confederates a dishonor, Colonel Shaw's father, Francis Shaw, proclaimed in a letter to Union Brigadier General Gillmore and to the regimental surgeon, Lincoln Stone, that he did not want his son's body returned stating, "We would not have his body removed from where it lies surrounded by his brave and devoted soldiers…We can imagine no holier place than that in which he lies, among his brave and devoted followers, nor wish for him better company – what a body-guard he has!"

As the word of the 54th Massachusetts bravery spread, Congress at last authorized the recruiting of black troops. Although the regiment was overwhelmed and driven back in the assault on Fort Wagner, Shaw's leadership and the valor of his unit, proved to be the turning point. The 54th's bravery dismissed any lingering skepticism about the combat readiness of African Americans.

Their bravery inspired thousands of African-Americans to enlist for the Union and contribute to its eventual victory. 180,000 men volunteered. President Lincoln credited those men of color with helping turn the tide of war. Ulysses S. Grant wrote to Lincoln saying, "I have given the subject of arming the Negro my hearty support. They will make good soldiers and taking them from the enemy weakens him in the same proportion they strengthen us."

Colonel Robert Gould Shaw, the son of a wealthy Boston abolitionist family, embodied a clear and deep commitment to his regiment, hoping to lead them in their fight to freedom. He said, "I wanted my men to fight by the side of whites, and they have done it." Shaw with the colonel's insignia of eagles on his army epaulets on July 18, 1863, marched into history forever with his beloved 54th Massachusetts Volunteers.

Colonel Robert Gould Shaw, May, 1863. Commander of the 54th Massachusetts Volunteers. (Oct. 10, 1837 – July 18, 1863) Courtesy of Library of Congress

Shaw's leadership passed into legend with a unit that inspired tens of thousands more African-Americans to enlist for the Union and contribute to its ultimate victory. circa 1863. Courtesy of Library of Congress

Full length portrait of Lieutenant Robert G. Shaw, 1861. Shaw was the son of a prominent Boston abolitionist family. Courtesy of Library of Congress.

Colonel Robert G. Shaw accepted command of the first all-black regiment in the Northeast. circa 1863. Courtesy of the Library of Congress.

A regiment of African-American Union Army soldiers poses for group photograph.
From Wikimedia Commons.

Men of Company E. 4th United States Colored Infantry Volunteers.
Courtesy of Library of Congress.

The gallant charge of the 54th Massachusettts Regiment and the death of Colonel Shaw, July 1863.
Courtesy of New York Public Library

Robert Gould Shaw Memorial, Boston, Massachusetts, 1900.
Courtesy of Library of Congress.

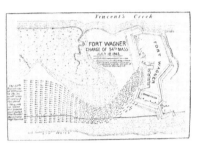

Showing General Butler who first coined the term "contrabands of war" applied to slaves freed by the Union army. Courtesy of N.Y. Public Library.

Map of the charge of the 54th Massachusetts on Fort Wagner, July 18, 1863. From Wikimedia Commons.

Peter Walton, Photographer, May 1863 – Sept. 1948

The First Black Recipient
Of The Medal Of Honor

WILLIAM HARVEY CARNEY WAS THE first African American to earn the prestigious Congressional Medal of Honor. As the highest military decoration awarded to members of the armed services, the Medal of Honor is reserved exclusively for those who perform acts of heroism so great that they are far more likely to die than survive. Sixteen African American men received the award during their Civil War service.

Carney's medal was not authorized until May 23, 1900. It was not unusual for acts of valor accomplished during the Civil War to go unrecognized for many years. Over half of the medals awarded during that time period, were not conferred till twenty or more years after the Civil War.

Carney was born a slave in Norfolk, Virginia, on February 29, 1840. According to most accounts he made his way to freedom along the Underground Railroad. At the age of twenty-three, Carney enlisted and trained with the newly created 54th Massachusetts Colored Infantry, the first all-black regiment authorized by Congress. Much depended on the 54th in battle if other regiments were to be raised.

Carney's mark in history came on July 18, 1863, during the 54th Massachusetts Volunteers' assault on Fort Wagner in Charleston, South Carolina. During the battle when the color guard was fatally wounded, Carney retrieved the flag and planted the colors at the top of the fort's parapet. Carney later said, "Nothing that any of us has ever done, was as important as this. We were fighting for all the black men and we could not fail." For his bravery beyond the call of duty, Carney was promoted to sergeant and granted several honors for gallant and meritorious conduct. Carney received an honorable discharge, due to the lingering effects of his wounds, in June, 1864.

The regiment's heroism had a ripple effect. It galvanized thousands of other black men to join the Union Army. With every marching step and round fired, none felt more keenly the purpose of the mission than the African American soldier. Even Abraham Lincoln noted that the 54th's bravery at Fort Wagner, was a key development that helped secure victory for the North.

Nearly 180,000 African American freedmen and runaway slaves have been documented to have served in the Union Army during the Civil War. They suffered casualties that were 35-50% greater than that of white soldiers. The African-American soldiers fought in every major campaign from 1864 to 1865.

Sergeant William Harvey Carney was the first Black American recommended for the Congressional Medal of Honor for extraordinary heroism on July 18, 1863.
Photo credit: U.S. Army

William Carney fought to protect one of the United State's greatest symbols during the Civil War—the American flag. He stated he fought to serve "my country and my oppressed brothers."
Photo credit: U.S. Army.

The 54th Massachusetts storm the parapet of Fort Wagner in Charleston, South Carolina. Photo credit: U.S. Army.

Carney supports himself with a cane as he holds the 54th's United States Army battle worn flag. Photo courtesy of the Congressional Medal of Honor Society.

Congressional Medal of Honor given to Sergeant William H. Carney for rallying the troops and saving the regimental colors. He was awarded the medal on May 23, 1900. Photo credit: Carl J. Cruz Collection.

In March 1863, William Harvey Carney joined the U.S. Army and was attached to Company C, 54th Massachusetts Colored Infantry Regiment. Photo Courtesy of Library of Congress.

"The Old Flag Never Touched the Ground." From: Wikimedia Commons.

The 54th attacking Fort Wagner (From Granger Collection). Photo credit: U.S. Army

The Amendments To The United States Constitution

Amendment 13: In 1865, the Thirteenth Amendment did away with slavery.

Section 1. Neither slavery nor involuntary servitude, except as a punishment or crime whereof the party shall have been duly convicted, shall exist within the United States, or any place subject to their jurisdiction.

Section 2. Congress shall have power to enforce this article by appropriate legislation.

Amendment 14: In 1868, the Fourteenth Amendment said that all persons born in the United States were citizens of the United States and no state could take away the rights given to them by the United States Constitution.

Section 1. All persons born or naturalized in the United States, and subject to the jurisdiction thereof, are citizens of the United States and the State wherein they reside. No State shall make or enforce any law which shall abridge the privileges or immunities of citizens of the United States; nor shall any State deprive any person of life, liberty, or property, without due process of law; nor deny to any person within its jurisdiction the equal protection of the laws.

Amendment 15: In 1870, the Fifteenth Amendment said no citizen could have their rights taken away from them because of race, color, or because they had once been a slave.

Section 1. The right of citizens of the United States to vote shall not be denied or abridged by the United States or by any State on account of race, color, or previous condition of servitude.

Section 2. The Congress shall have the power to enforce this article by appropriate legislation.

Citations

Throughout *Out of Slavery: A Novel of Harriet Tubman*, I have normalized the plantation dialect used by previous biographers when quoting Harriet Tubman and others. I am unsure of the accuracy of the recordings of her particular speech patterns.

Preface

"During the evening of November 12, 1833": Pratt, John P. "Spectacular Meteor Shower Might Repeat," *Meridian Magazine*, October 15, 1999.

"And then, we saw the lightning and that was the guns": Hart, Albert Bushnell, *Slavery and Abolition 1811-1841, The American Nation: A History* (New York: Harper & Brothers Publishers, 1906), 16:209.

"Free speech and slavery could not coexist": Kraditor, Aileen, *Means and Ends in Abolitionism: Garrison and His Critics on Strategy and Tactics, 1834-1850* (New York: Pantheon Books, 1967) p. 62.

"History was not merely an entity altered by the passage of time": Blight, David W., *For Something Beyond the Battlefield*, The Journal of American History, Vol. 75, No.4 (Mar., 1989), p. 1177.

Chapter 1: Uprooted

"I'll use this (pistol) and you will": Bradford, *Harriet Tubman: the Moses of her People*, p 33.

"When I found I had crossed that line for the first time": Bradford, *Scenes in the Life*, p. 20.

"I wouldn't be trusting Uncle Sam": Bradford, *Harriet Tubman: the Moses of her People*, p. 39.

"When I learned that my master was going to send me south": Bradford, *Harriet Tubman: the Moses of Her People*, p. 26.

"I was free but there was no one to welcome me": Bradford, *Scenes*, p. 20.

"But the difference ... Most that I have done": Bradford, *Harriet Tubman: the Moses of Her People*, p. 135.

"I have had the applause of the crowd": Bradford, *Harriet Tubman: the Moses of Her People*, p. 135.

Chapter 2: Stings of Slavery

"Harriet you have worked for others long enough": Bradford, *Harriet Tubman: the Moses of Her People*, p. 89.

"I've heard Uncle Tom's Cabin read": Taylor, *Harriet Tubman: Antislavery Activist*, p. 63.

"I've hear the shrieks and cries of women": Bradford, *Harriet Tubman: the Moses of Her People*, p. 15.

"Every time I saw a white man I was afraid": Benjamin Drew, The Refuge: *A North-Side View of Slavery* (1855 reprint, Tilden 116 G. Edelstein, ed., Reading, Mass: Addison-Wesley Publishing Co., 1969) p. 20.

"I listened many times to the groaned out": Bradford, *Scenes*, p. 14.

"I prayed to God to make me strong and able to fight": Cheney, *Moses*, p. 34.

"The plantation cook and I went to a nearby store": Bradford, *Scenes*, p. 74.

"That was the last thing I remembered": Telford, Emma P., *Harriet: The Moses of Heroism and Visions*, p. 5-6.

"No one would even pay a sixpence for me:" Bradford, *Scenes*, p 13-14.

"Oh dear Lord, I ain't got no friend but you": Bradford, *Harriet Tubman: the Moses of Her People*, p. 32.

"After a long illness, a deep religious spirit": Bradford, *Harriet Tubman: the Moses of Her People*, p. 24-25.

"My cry to slaveholders has always been": Bradford, *Harriet Tubman: the Moses of Her People*, p. 3.

"I think slavery is the next thing to hell. If a person would": Bradford, *Scenes in the Life of Harriet Tubman*, (Auburn: New York: W. J. Moses, 1869), p. 20.

"Now I've been free, I know what a dreadful condition slavery": Quarles, Benjamin. *"Harriet Tubman's Unlikely Leadership"*, Litwick, Leon, *Black Leaders of the Nineteenth Century*, (Chicago: University of Illinois Press, 1988) p. 43.

"A strong vision came to me in a dream": Bradford, *Harriet Tubman: the Moses of Her People*, p. 26.

"I realized that freedom did not guarantee": Bradford, *Scenes in the Life of Harriet Tubman*, (Auburn: New York: W. J. Moses, 1869) p. 20.

"On many rescue missions, my last stop": Bradford, *Harriet Tubman: the Moses of Her People*, p. 44.

"Slaves on plantations must not be seen": Bradford, *Harriet Tubman: the Moses of Her People*, p. 27.

"I'd sing familiar hymns:" Bradford, *Harriet Tubman: the Moses of Her People*, p. 28.

"One time I received news that my father": Thomas Garret to Mary Edmundson, August 11, 1857, in McGowan, *Station Master*, p. 143-45.

"I found an old horse": Bradford, *Scenes*, p. 52.

"There is a parable about a farmer": "New England Convention of Colored Citizens," *The Liberator,* Boston, August 26, 1859.

"I did not take up the work for my own benefit": "Dedication of Harriet Tubman's Home," *Auburn Daily Advertiser*, Auburn, N.Y., June 24, 1908; "Tubman Open and Aged Harriet Was Central Figure of the Celebration," Auburn Citizen, Auburn, N.Y., June 24, 1908.

"On one of my journeys, there were a number": Bradford, *Harriet Tubman: the Moses of Her People*, p. 74.

"On another journey south, a party of fugitive slaves": Bradford, *Harriet Tubman: the Moses of Her People*, p. 91.

"I said to the Lord, I'm going to hold steady": Bradford, *Harriet Tubman: the Moses of Her People*, p. 61.

"Another time, I felt compelled to go down": Bradford, *Harriet Tubman: the Moses of Her People*, p. 79.

"John saw the city. He saw twelve gates": Bradford, *Harriet Tubman: the Moses of Her People*, p. 79.

"God was always near. He gave me the strength": Cheney, *Moses*, p. 34.

"I never knew a time when I did not trust": Bradford, *Harriet Tubman: the Moses of Her People*, p. 23.

"When folks were given praise, I'd say": Bradford, *Harriet Tubman: the Moses of Her People*, p. 61.

"God will take up others": "Dedication of Harriet Tubman's Home," *Auburn Daily Advertiser*, Auburn, N.Y., June 24, 1908; "Tubman Open and Aged Harriet Was Central Figure of the Celebration," Auburn Citizen, Auburn, N.Y., June 24, 1908.

"Come up higher": Bradford, *Harriet Tubman: the Moses of Her People*, p. 131.

Chapter 3: Way down South in Dixie:

"Harriet didn't know exactly how, but she says": Bradford, *Scenes* p. 50-51. Thomas Garret to Sarah Bradford, June 1868.

"Peace, peace as much as they like, but I know": Bradford, *Harriet Tubman: the Moses of Her People*, p. 115.

"Harriet, would you be willing and act as a spy": Bradford, *Harriet Tubman: the Moses of Her People*, p. 93-94.

"They laugh when they hear me talk, and I": Bradford, *Harriet Tubman: the Moses of Her People*, p. 103.

"I get a big chunk of ice and put it into a basin": Bradford, *Scenes*, p. 37.

"The first man I come to, I thrash away the flies": Bradford, *Scenes*, p. 37.

"God won't let Master Lincoln beat the South": Lydia Maria Child to John G. Whittier, January 21, 1862. Lydia Maria Child Papers, Library of Congress, Washington D.C.

"The frightened plantation slaves saw the gunboats": Bradford, *Harriet Tubman: the Moses of Her People*, p. 99-100.

"On hearing the ship's whistle, they ran down": Bradford, *Harriet Tubman: the Moses of Her People*, p. 99.

"Colonel Montgomery shouted from the upper": Bradford, *Harriet Tubman: the Moses of Her People,* p. 101.

"Of all the whole creation in the East and the West": Bradford, *Harriet Tubman: the Moses of Her People,* p. 102.

"The only woman led armed men into battle": Lawson, *Harriet Tubman: Bound for the Promised Land*, Introduction p. xviii.

Chapter 4: Climbing Jacob's Ladder

"To me the idea fighting the South without": Douglass, Frederick, *Fighting Rebels with Only one Hand*, Douglass Monthly, September, 1861. (Foner, Vol. 3, pages 151-154).

"Let us win for ourselves the gratitude of our country": Douglass, Frederick, *"Men of Color to Arms!"* Speech, March 3, 1863. www. loc.gov/resource/mfd.22005/?sp=1

"Once let the black man get upon his person the brass": Douglass, Frederick, Address at a Meeting for the Proclamation of Colored Enlistments, *The Elected Speeches of Frederick Douglass*, www.loc. gov/resource/mfd.22007/?sp=1

"The day dawns; the morning sun is bright upon the horizon,"

Douglass, Frederick, *"Men of Color to Arms!"* Speech, March 3, 1863. www.loc.gov/resource/mfd.22005/?sp=1

"A black man's life is worth the same as a": Werstein, *The Storming of Fort Wagner: Black Valor in the Civil War,* p. 83.

"Men of Color, to Arms!:" Douglass, Frederick. March 3, 1863. Manuscript/Mixed Material. Retrieved from the Library of Congress, <www.loc.gov/item/mfd.22005/>

Chapter 5: Wishing

"If he could do without me, then I could do without him": Cheney, "Moses" p. 35.

Chapter 6: Harriet and the Colonel

"Harriet cooked Colonel Robert Gould Shaw's last meal:" Taylor, Robert W. *Harriet Tubman: Heroine in Ebony, p. 13.*

Chapter 7: Saving Old Glory

"There will be almost no one left alive": Werstein, The Storming of Fort Wagner: Black Valor in the Civil War, p. 96.

"Boys, I only did my duty; the old flag never:" Carney, William Harvey, (1840-1908)". The Center for African American Genealogical Research, Inc. Retrieved 1 March 2015.

"And then, we saw the lightning and that was the guns": Hart, Albert Bushnell, *Slavery and Abolition 1811-1841, The American*

Nation: A History (New York: Harper & Brothers Publishers, 1906), 16:209.

Chapter 9: Roses at the Racecourse

"I will bury him in a common trench": Luis F. Emilio, *History of the Fifty-Fourth Regiment.* (Boston: The Boston Company, 1894).

"We can imagine no holier place": Luis F. Emilio, *A Brave Black Regiment.* Boston: 1894, pp. 102-103.

Chapter 10: Cookies with Harriet

"When I was in Boston": Bradford, Sarah, *Moses,* (1901) p. 152-153.

"I had great confidence that God would protect": Garret to Wigham, December 27, 1856, in McGowan, *Station Master,* 134-138.

"I was a conductor on the Underground Railroad": Holt, *Heroine* p. 426.

"Three years before while staying one night": Bradford, Sarah. *Harriet Tubman: the Moses of her People,* p. 92-93.

"Later Sojourner Truth met President Lincoln": Holt, *Heroine* p. 426.

"I was given leave from my army position": Martha Coffin Wright to Marianna Pelham Wright, November 7, 1865, Garrison Family Papers, Sophia Smith Garrison, Smith College, North Hampton, Massachusetts. Bradford, Scenes, p.46.

"I felt like a blackberry in pail of white milk": Bradford, *Harriet* (1901), p. 149-50.

"I'm going to go home to tell Lord Jesus": Bradford, *Harriet* (1901), p. 150.

Chapter 11: Touched by Harriet's Great Heart

"Singing Swing, Low Sweet Chariot": Conrad, *Harriet Tubman*, p. 224.

"One of the last times Harriet attended church": Conrad, *Harriet Tubman*, p. 223

"She has brought the two races nearer together": Conrad, *Harriet Tubman*, p. 225.

"There is only one more journey for me to take": Bradford, *Harriet Tubman: the Moses of Her People*, p. 53.

"I go away to prepare a place for you": "Death of Aunt Harriet, Moses of Her People," *Auburn Daily Advertiser*, Auburn, N.Y., March 11, 1913.

"When I was about to leave, Harriet reached for": Burns, *Harriet Tubman: And the Fight Against Slavery*. New York, p. 71.

"Do you really believe that women should vote?:" Clark, James B., "*An Hour with Harriet Tubman,*" in Christophe: A Tragedy of Prose of Imperial Hatti, 1911.

"Tubman was to work in a private way for activities": Bradford, *Harriet Tubman: the Moses of Her People*, p. 135.

"Governor Seward wrote of her": Bradford, *Harriet Tubman: The Moses of Her People*, p. 77.

"Queen Victoria of England read her": Clark, James B. *"An Hour with Harriet Tubman: in Christophe: A Tragedy of in Prose of Imperial Haiti"* ed. William Edgar Easton (Los Angeles: Grafton Publishing Co. 1911).

She blamed it on the way those master were brought up, with the whip in their hands." Conrad, *Harriet Tubman*, p. 10.

"The terrible winter of 1867 – 1868": Bradford, *Scenes*, p. 112.

"Put on the large pot, we're going to have soup tonight": *Harriet Tubman: the Moses of Her People*, (New York: J.J. Little & Co., 1901), p.143.

"I never met any person, any color, who had": Bradford, *Harriet Tubman: the Moses of Her People*, p. 83.

"Harriet's prayer was a prayer of faith": Bradford, *Harriet Tubman: the Moses of Her People*, p. 57.

"I have known Harriet a long time, and a nobler": Bradford, *Harriet Tubman: the Moses of Her People*, p. 76.

"Some have said of the legendary Underground Railroad and its secret system"; *Underground Railroad*, National Park Service, p. 45-46.

About Harriet Tubman

"Harriet suffered under the lash and rose above": Lawson, *Bound for the Promised Land*, p. 53.

"She was a witness to some of the most horrific fighting": Taylor, *A Black Woman's Civil War Memories*, p. 68.

"One June 1, 1863, she was the first and only women": Lawson, *Bound for the Promised Land*, Introduction, and p. xviii.

The First Memorial Day

"In Charleston, South Carolina, where the war had begun": Blight, *Race and Reunion*, p.65.

"During the final year of the war, the Confederate command": Blight, *Race and Reunion*, p. 68.

"Among the Union troops to enter Charleston and receive its surrender": Blight, *Race and Reunion* p. 66, Robert N. Rosen, Confederate Charleston.

"A New York Tribune called it 'a procession of friends and mourners": *New York Tribune*, May 13, 1865.

"The war was over, and Memorial Day had been founded": Blight, *Race and Reunion,* p. 70.

"The war was not just a struggle of mere sectional character": Douglass. Speech at Memorial Service in New York, 1878.

"By their labor and their words, and their solemn parade": Blight, *Race and Reunion: the Civil War in American Memory*, p. 70.

Colonel Robert G. Shaw and the
54th Massachusetts Volunteers

"Shaw's father's letter": From Lois F. Emilio, A Brave Regiment, Boston, 1894, pp. 102-103.

"I have given the subject of arming the Negro my hearty support": Personal Memories of Ulysses S. Grant: Memoirs and Selected Letters, Literary Classics of the United States, Inc., New York, N.Y., 1990, p. 1031.

"I wanted my men to fight by the side of whites, and they have done it." Memorial Robert Gould Shaw, Cambridge: University Press, 1864.

William H. Carney – The First Black Recipient of the Meal of Honor

"Nothing any of us has ever done before, was as": Werstein, *The Storming of Fort Wagner: Black Valor in the Civil War*, p. 54.

References

Blight, David W. *Race and Reunion: The Civil War in American History.* Cambridge, Massachusetts: Belknap Press of Harvard University Press, 2001.

Bradford, Sarah H. *Harriet Tubman: The Moses of Her People.* Bedford, Massachusetts: Applewood Books, 1886.

Bradford, Sarah H. *Scenes in the Life of Harriet Tubman,* Auburn, N.Y.: W. J. Moses, 1869.

Burns, Bree. *Harriet Tubman: And the Fight Against Slavery.* New York: Chelsea Juniors, 1992.

Clinton, Catherine. *Harriet Tubman: The Road to Freedom.* New York: Little, Brown and Company, 2004.

Conrad, Earl. Harriet Tubman. Washington, D.C.: Associated Publishers, 1943.

Duncan, Russell, editor. *Blue-Eyed Child of Fortune: The Civil War Letters Colonel Robert Gould Shaw.* Athens, Georgia: University of Georgia Press, 1992.

Epic Leaders: One Hundred Black Women Who Made a Difference. Detroit, Michigan: Visible Ink Press, 1993.

Garrison, Webb. *Amazing Women of the Civil War.* Nashville, Tennessee: Rutledge Hill Press, 1999.

Hall, Richard. *Patriots in Disguise: Women Warriors of the Civil War.* New York: Marlowe & Company, 1994.

Larson, Kate Clifford. *Bound for the Promised Land: Harriet Tubman, Portrait of an America Hero.* New York: One World, Random House Publishing Group, 2003.

Litwick, Leon and August Meir. *Black Leaders of the Nineteenth Century.* Chicago: University Press of Illinois, 1988.

McClard, Megan. *Harriet Tubman: Slavery and the Underground Railroad.* New Jersey: Silver Burdett Press, 1991.

Petry, Ann. *Harriet Tubman: Conductor on the Underground Railroad.* New York: Pocket Books, 1955.

Sadlier, Rosemary. *Harriet Tubman and the Underground Railroad: Her Life in the United States and Canada.* Toronto, Canada: Umbrella Press, 1997.

Sally, Columbus. *The Black 100: A Ranking of the Most Influential African-Americans, Past and Present.* New York: The Carol Publishing Group, 1993.

Siebert, Wilbur H. *The Underground Railroad: From Slavery to Freedom.* New York: Dover Publications, Inc., 2006.

Smith, Jessie Carney. *Epic Lives: One Hundred Black Women Who Made a Difference.* Detroit: Visible Ink Press. 1993.

Sullivan, George. *Harriet Tubman.* New York: Scholastic Books Inc., 2001.

Taylor, M.W. *Harriet Tubman: Antislavery Activist.* New York: Chelsea House Publishers, 1991.

Underground Railroad. Washington D.C.: Division of Publications, National Park Service, 1998.

Werstein, Irving. *The Storming of Fort Wagner: Black Valor in the Civil War.* New York: Firebird Books, 1970.

Internet Sources:

"The Battle over Shaw's Body." Past in the Present, 7 May 2017, https://pastinthepresent.wordpress.com/2017/07/19/the-battle-over-shaws-body/.

Coddington, Ronald S. "Robert Gould Shaw's Gruesome Task." *Opinionator,* New York Times, 12 Aug. 2012, opinionator.blogs.nytimes.com/2012/08/12/robert-gould-shaws-gruesome-task/.

Donnelly, Paul. "Harriet Tubman's Great Raid." *Opinionator,* 7 June 2013, www.opinionator.blogs.nytimes.com/2013/06/07/harriet-tubmans-great-raid/.

Gaskell, Elizabeth. "Robert Gould Shaw." *Macmillan's Magazine,* 1863, lang.nagoya-u.ac.jp/~matsuoka/EG-Shaw.html.

Hammond, Thomas M. "William H. Carney: 54h Massachusetts Soldier and First Black U.S. Medal of Honor Recipient." *American Civil War,* 29 Jan. 2007. historynet.com/william-h-carney-54th-massachusetts-soldier-and-first-black-us-medal-of-honor-recipient.htm.

"Harriet Tubman is Dead." *Memoriam,* 16 May 2016, harriettubman.com/index.html

Henig, Gerald S. "Glory at Battery Wagner." *Civil War Times,* 48.3, June 2009, p. 36. historynet.com/glory-battery-wagner.htm.

Janney, Rebecca Price. "People of Faith: Harriet Tubman." *Crosswalk,* 21 Feb. 2003, crosswalk.com/faith/spiritual-life/people-of-faith-harriet-tubman-1186786.html

Kashatus, William C. "America's Civil War: 54th Massachusetts Regiment." *American History Magazine*, Oct. 2000, historynet. com/americas-civil-war-54th-massachusetts-regiment.html.

Lamothe, Dan. "Harriet Tubman was more than an Underground Railroad icon. She was a Civil War spy." *Checkpoint*, 20 Apr. 2016, washingtonpost.com/news/checkpoint/wp/2016/04/20/harriet-tubman-was-more-than-an-underground-railroad-icon-she-was-a-civil-war-spy-hero/?noredirect=on&utm_term=.5b18f17dba23

Larson, Kate Clifford. "Bound for the Promised Land: Harriet Tubman Portrait of an American Hero." wwwharriettubmanbiography.com/

Lauderdale, David. "Memorials at Beaufort National Cemetery tell the lost story of America's first Memorial Day." 24 May 2015, www.islandpacket.com/news/local/community/beaufort-news/bg-military/article33649872.html/

"Robert Gould Shaw." May 2016, https://www.revolvy.com/topic/Robert%20Gould%20Shaw.

Velez, Denise Oliver. "The Memorial Day History Forgot: The Martyrs of the Race Course." *Daily Kos*, 28 May 2014, dailykos.com/stories/2018/5/28/1767621/-The-Memorial-Day-history-forgot-The-Martyrs-of-the-Race-Course.

About the Author

Carol is an Amazon bestselling author, speaker, and educator. She holds a Masters in Library and Information Science from Wayne State University and a Masters in Educational Technology from Michigan State University. Her mission is to bring more awareness about the life and times of Harriet Tubman—the heroine of the Underground Railroad.

CPSIA information can be obtained
at www.ICGtesting.com
Printed in the USA
FFHW020747150519
52459872-57876FF

9 780990 744689